The Bunker

Adam McKim

For Rob

Prologue

One year had passed since Earth suffered the devastating strike, and the government bunker now held over 200 survivors. Concrete walls that had once gleamed had grown dull and worn, though they continued to shield the occupants from the brutal, ravaged world outside. Fluorescent lights flickered overhead, casting an intermittent glow over the winding tunnels that linked various chambers within the bunker. The air was thick with low, murmured voices and the rhythmic echo of footsteps, weaving an atmosphere of cautious camaraderie among the people.

A determined and just leader, Emily Stone moved

with purpose through one of the main corridors, her gaze scanning the crowd steadily. Selected by the citizens to guide them, she bore her role steadfastly, determined to uphold the safety and welfare of those who had trusted her. The weight of this responsibility pressed heavily on her, but she carried it with a quiet dignity, intent on creating order and hope in their confined, subterranean world.

A diligent researcher, David Chen worked hard at the heart of the bunker's operations. His role focused on assessing radiation levels on the surface, a task essential to everyone's future safety. He conducted meticulous weekly tests, ensuring the bunker's barriers held firm against the residual radiation above. His devotion to his work was undeniable, but frustration gnawed at him. Despite his endless testing, the levels outside remained hazardous, prolonging their confinement and leaving him restless in the face of unchanging danger.

Frank Johnson, once a beat cop in the bustling streets above ground, now held the title of head of security. Walking intently through the maze-like tunnels, Frank upheld his duty with the same resolve he'd once shown patrolling the city. He was responsible for preserving order within the bunker, where tensions ran high, and space was scarce. Although his role had changed, his dedication to protecting the citizens remained unshaken, and his presence inspired trust amid the crowded halls.

Dr. Sarah Thompson worked tirelessly in a modest clinic to treat the many residents needing care. Her compassion for her patients shone through despite the challenges of her work. Resources were limited, and even minor illnesses became difficult to treat in the bunker's restricted environment. Despite the relentless demands, Sarah never wavered; her persistence in the face of overwhelming odds inspired the community, who admired her unwavering dedication to their well-being.

Meanwhile, Robert Green tended to the hydroponic gardens that provided the only source of fresh food for the bunker's inhabitants. Quiet and focused, Robert managed the complex system of pipes and pumps with meticulous care, nurturing the plants with a calm efficiency that belied the importance of his work. These gardens provided a vital sense of life and hope for the community, and Robert's commitment to his role was evident in the thriving greenery that flourished under his steady watch.

Daily life within the bunker was fraught with challenges, and the pressure wore heavily on everyone.

Cramped quarters and limited resources fueled an ever-present frustration, and though they longed to return to the surface, they knew that it remained too dangerous. Yet, in the face of this hardship, the community held together, clinging to the hope of someday seeing the sky again. Until then, they persevered, united in their resolve to survive in this harsh, underground world.

Amidst this constant struggle, Jack, the bunker's lead engineer, worked tirelessly behind the scenes, keeping the bunker's vital systems running smoothly. A quiet figure, Jack found solace in the hum of the machines, his presence a grounding force within the bunker. His work was indispensable; with his unyielding maintenance, the bunker would continue. Jack bore the weight of this responsibility with a steady determination, knowing the lives of those within these walls rested on his skill and dedication.

* * *

David sat alone at his desk, scrutinizing several weeks' radiation data. Scanning the latest readings, his eyes caught a surprising trend: the radiation levels were falling faster than he had ever seen before. A wave of excitement surged through him as the realization struck him. Earth was healing. This change meant the planet was recovering faster than anyone had dared hope. The prospect of returning to the surface was no longer a distant dream but an approaching possibility.

Without hesitation, David gathered his notes and hurried to Emily's office, his heart pounding with urgency and excitement. Bursting in, he barely caught his breath as he announced, "Emily, I have incredible news."

"What is it, David?" she replied, her curiosity rose.

"The levels have dropped dramatically over the past months," David said. "At this rate, there is a possibility we could return to the surface in a year, give or take a month or two."

Emily was taken aback, absorbing the news in quiet astonishment. She had seen the disappointment and frustration in the eyes of those forced to live in these tight quarters for so long. The thought of returning above ground was an impossible hope they had all but let go of. Yet David's discovery offered a glimmer of real promise.

"David, are you sure about this?" she asked.

"Emily, I've double-checked everything. The decline is unmistakable," he replied.

The enormity of this revelation weighed on Emily.

As a leader, she knew she was responsible for confirming the information before sharing it with the people. Raising their hopes without certainty could do more harm than good.

"We must handle this carefully," she said, her voice steady but cautious. "We can't risk giving the people false hope. Keep this information confidential for now. We don't want anyone to become overly hopeful until we know for sure."

David nodded, understanding her caution, though his excitement lingered. "I'll keep running checks, Emily. If anything changes, I'll let you know."

"Good," she replied.

Chapter 1

One Year Earlier

Emily's hands trembled as she gripped the remote. Her eyes locked on the TV. The show she'd been watching cut to black, and bold letters filled the screen:

ATTENTION! CRITICAL ANNOUNCEMENT OF MASS DESTRUCTION

A chill ran down her spine. Her pulse quickened as her thoughts whirled—what could warrant a message like this? Then, the President appeared, his face drawn and serious. Emily braced herself.

"My fellow Americans and people of the world,"

the President began, his voice heavy with sorrow. "I come to you with a heavy heart to deliver news of grave concern. For the past several months, my administration and world leaders have closely monitored a series of asteroids on a collision course with our planet. Despite every effort, we've been unable to stop or deflect them."

He paused, taking a deep breath before he continued. "These asteroids are larger than we first estimated, and their impact will have catastrophic consequences. They will strike locations across the globe, unleashing unimaginable destruction. Some of these asteroids are on course to hit a region housing a large nuclear arsenal. This impact will trigger a massive nuclear explosion and release radioactive material into the atmosphere. The devastation will be beyond anything we've ever known."

Emily's heart hammered as she listened, her face paling. She clutched the remote, unable to tear her eyes from the screen. Her mind raced, grasping at the enormity of what she was hearing. This was no drill, no passing threat—it was the end of everything they knew. "The impact is expected in two days," the President continued, his voice trembling slightly. "I implore each of you to seek immediate shelter. The situation is dire, but we must come together as a global community to do all we can to mitigate the effects of this tragedy."

The President's face filled with a grim resolve as he continued. "I know this news is difficult to accept, but I ask for your courage and resilience. This may be the end of the world as we know it, yet I have faith in the strength and resiliency of the human spirit. I bid you farewell and hope we can rise to this great challenge."

Emily's mind spun in disbelief. She never imagined living through such a disaster, and the sheer helplessness of it all was crushing. She glanced out her window, where streets teemed with panicked people, their voices and shouts filling the air. A wave of despair washed over her as she backed away, stumbling into the bathroom.

Shutting the door, she leaned against the wall for a moment, her body wracked with emotions. Slowly, she undressed, tossing her clothes aside, and stepped into the shower. Turning on the faucet, she let the steaming water wash over her, hoping the heat might soothe her spiraling thoughts. As the water streamed down her face, so did her tears.

Memories of her life flooded her head as if the shower was pouring them all over her. Everything she had worked hard for in her life was now swirling down the drain. She had no family nearby to turn to. A few years ago, she had moved to the city, leaving them hundreds of miles away. Now, standing alone, she felt more isolated than ever, surrounded by a world that was swiftly unraveling. The end was upon them, and there was nowhere to run.

* * *

David sat at his desk, his gaze unfocused as he stared blankly at his computer. A sense of dread washed over him as he recalled the President's words. Just then, a knock sounded at his door, snapping him out of despair. He rose slowly, his limbs heavy, and opened the door to find two Secret Service agents standing before him.

"David Chen, we need you to come with us," one of the agents said.

David looked at them, confusion flickering across his face. "Why? What's going on?"

"Your skills are required in a secure location. The government needs your expertise," the other agent explained.

David glanced back into his home. "Can I bring my wife with me?"

The agents exchanged glances, and then one

replied, "I'm sorry, Mr. Chen, but our orders are specific. We're only authorized to take you."

Just then, his wife, Mary, appeared in the doorway, worry etched on her face. "David? What's going on?" she asked, her eyes darting between him and the agents.

"Everything's fine, Mary," he said, sounding reassuring. But as he turned back to the agents, his face hardened. "I won't leave without her. She's my wife. I can't abandon her."

The agents' expressions remained unyielding. "We understand, Mr. Chen, but our orders are clear. There's nothing we can do. You need to come with us now."

David clenched his hands into fists, his anger simmering. He wouldn't be bullied by anyone, not even the government. "I'm not going anywhere without her," he replied, his voice trembling with defiance.

One of the agents stepped forward, his tone stern. "Mr. Chen, we don't have much time. The asteroids will hit in two days. We need you to monitor the radiation levels in the coming months."

David felt the desperation welling within him, but he refused to leave. "Again, I'm not going without her," he insisted.

Suddenly, the agents seized him, and before he knew it, he was being pulled from his doorway.

"David, no!" Mary cried, reaching for him.

"Stay back, Mary!" he shouted. "Agents, please— don't do this!"

But his protests fell on deaf ears. As he was taken farther away from her, he couldn't shake the sinking feeling that he might never see her again.

* * *

Frank Johnson gripped the steering wheel of his patrol car, the weight of his role pressing down on him as his radio crackled with the President' s announcement. He'd known the situation was grave, but hearing it laid out in such stark terms felt like a punch to the gut. Soon, the streets would be chaos, and he was tasked with maintaining order.

As he drove, the panic around him was already evident. People ran in every direction, cars stuck in a cacophony of honks, and emergency sirens wailed. The situation unraveled quickly, and he knew he was only one man. There was no way he could stop this kind of madness.

"Frank, come in," his supervisor's voice barked over the radio, dragging him from his thoughts. "What's your status?"

He hesitated, his thoughts drifting to his wife and daughter. He couldn't stand the idea of being separated from them in the face of this disaster.

"Frank, do you copy?" his supervisor repeated, more urgently this time.

"Yes, sir," Frank replied, his voice low.

"Stay on the streets and keep things under control," his supervisor ordered. "We need every available unit."

Frank took a deep breath, his responsibility bearing down on him. But he couldn't ignore the pull of his family, the urge to protect them, to be by their side when the worst hit. "I'm sorry, sir. I can't."

"Frank!" his supervisor barked, his voice echoing with frustration.

But Frank had made up his mind. "I have to go," he said quietly, switching off the radio before he could hear any more.

He drove home as fast as he could, weaving through the growing chaos around him. When he arrived at his house, he found his wife, Jane, and their daughter, Lily, frantically packing bags.

"Jane! Lily! We need to go now!" he called out.

Jane's eyes widened, her face going pale. "What are we going to do?"

"We have to find shelter," Frank replied. "Lily,

sweetie, grab whatever you need. We're leaving."

Just eight years old, Lily nodded tearfully, running to her room to gather her things.

As they packed, Jane turned to him, her voice wavering. "Where are we going to go, Frank?"

He paused, his uncertainty clear. "I don't know. But we must get out of the city. We have to find someplace safe."

Jane nodded, tears streaming down her face. She reached for his hand, and he squeezed it. They packed the car and left their house behind. As Frank drove through the panicked streets, he glanced at his family. They had each other, and that was all they could hold on to.

Chapter 2

Emily sat on the edge of her seat, breath suspended, as she tuned into the latest updates on the asteroids. The President's announcement had kept her awake all night, and now, with only a day left until impact, she was still grappling with the full extent of the crisis. The chaos unfolding on the streets outside mirrored the images on the TV screen: people rioting and looting in a frantic attempt to find supplies.

"Breaking news!" the anchorman's voice boomed over the speakers. "We're receiving reports of a massive crowd gathering around one of the government's designated bunkers. This bunker had been closed for years but was reopened in response to the current situation."

The screen cut to a shaky feed of people pressing toward a bunker entrance, tension clear.

"Word spread fast about this previously abandoned bunker, and crowds have begun to arrive. The army is on the scene, working to keep control, but they're vastly outnumbered by the sheer number of people and the last-minute decision to reopen it. We have confirmation that the bunker doors remain open as soldiers attempt to admit selected individuals."

Emily's mind raced as she grasped the gravity of the situation. This could be her last chance for survival. She grabbed her keys and dashed out the door. Once in the car, she tuned into the radio, hoping for more updates on the situation.

"Can you describe the scene for us?" the host asked.

"It's madness," replied an eyewitness. "People are pushing and shoving, desperate to get inside."

Emily felt her heart sink as she listened. Did she even have a chance with all those people there? There was only one way to find out. She tightened her grip on the wheel and floored the pedal.

* * *

The two Secret Service agents escorted David down the bunker's hall, their expressions tense. The chaos outside could be heard even within the bunker, the crowd's desperate pleas and shouts echoing through the halls.

"What's being done to help these people find shelter?" David asked the agents, his voice edged with frustration.

"In the event of total world destruction, only the top minds in the world are saved to try to rebuild," one agent explained. "It's a carefully selected group to ensure the future of humankind."

"That's not right," David replied, his frustration intensifying. "The government should have prepared shelters for everyone. These people are who they work for. Do you know that Switzerland has enough bunkers to shelter its entire population?"

The agents nodded. "Yes, but this isn't Switzerland; it's America. Unfortunately, this is the protocol we have to follow."

David exhaled a heavy sigh. "Switzerland got it right. It's a shame other countries aren't taking the necessary measures to protect their citizens."

The agents exchanged a brief look, unsure of how to respond. They continued in silence, the sound of the desperate crowd outside lingering as a harsh reminder of their reality.

David was led to the bunker's core, where General Michaels awaited him.

"Mr. Chen," General Michaels began, his voice steady, "I've been informed that you're crucial to our mission. Your expertise in monitoring fallout and radiation risks is vital to ensuring humanity's survival during a global disaster."

As the General spoke, David's thoughts drifted to his wife, who was left behind and vulnerable to the impending catastrophe. He interrupted, "What about my wife, General? Can she join us?"

General Michaels sighed, his expression pained. "I understand your concern, Mr. Chen, but there are no exceptions. Allowing your wife would set a precedent, and soon, others would demand the same treatment. We don't have the resources."

But David was resolute. "My skills are only valuable if she's with me."

The room fell silent as General Michaels considered his options. He knew how critical David's expertise was, yet he also understood the implications of making exceptions. After a moment of contemplation, he nodded.

"Very well, Mr. Chen. We'll make arrangements for your wife to join us. But know that this isn't out of kindness. If I could replace you with someone equally qualified, you and your wife would be left outside. The fate of humanity is at stake. Don't lose sight of that."

As David was shown to his quarters, relief washed over him. Though the decision about his wife's safety had been burdensome to the General, he was thankful for the chance to use his skills for humanity's future. He settled into his quarters, prepared for the challenges that lay ahead.

* * *

Frank navigated the chaotic streets, struggling to remain calm as danger swirled around them. His wife, Jane, sat beside him, her eyes wide as she watched the turmoil outside. Their daughter, Lily, huddled in the backseat, her face etched with fear.

"Frank, where are we going to find shelter?" Jane asked.

"I don't know," he replied, gripping the wheel tightly.

They tuned into the radio, catching the broadcast about the gathering crowd outside the government bunker.

"Frank, we need to go there," Jane urged. "It might be our only chance."

Frank hesitated, fully aware of the risks of confronting government forces during such a critical time. The earth's destruction was imminent, and the stakes were unbearably high.

"Jane, it's dangerous," Frank said. "We could get hurt."

"We need to see what the situation is like," Jane insisted. "We have to protect Lily."

Lily, quiet in the backseat, looked up. "Dad, I'm scared. What's happening?"

Frank glanced back at her. "It's okay, Lily. We're finding somewhere safe. I won't let anything happen to you."

Jane's pleading eyes met his once more. "Please, Frank. We have to try."

He let out a resigned sigh and nodded. "Alright, we'll go see. But I can't promise anything."

Frank turned the car around and drove in the direction of the bunker, uncertain of what lay ahead but determined to protect his family.

* * *

As Emily drove toward the bunker, her mind whirled with thoughts of the government's lack of preparation for its citizens. She felt a surge of anger, her thoughts racing. How could the government—and world leaders—have kept such a massive secret? Why hadn't they built shelters to protect the population? Announcing the asteroids before securing the bunkers and locking the doors was a massive error.

Chaos reigned as people fought for survival while the government scrambled to protect only a few. The situation was dire, and she knew the people wouldn't stand for it. They would fight with everything they had. As she approached the bunker, Emily saw the crowds pushing forward, desperate to get inside. Soldiers stood guard, but it was a losing battle. The frantic and angry people wouldn't back down until they found safety.

Taking a deep breath, Emily steeled herself. She was determined to survive and wouldn't let anyone stop her. She would join the crowd and fight her way to safety if that's what it took.

Chapter 3

As Emily approached the gate to the bunker, the scene ahead was even more chaotic than expected. People were crushed together, shouting and pressing forward desperately to get closer to the entrance. Panic was thick in the air, filling her senses. Every voice around her screamed in anger or fear while others tried to bargain, their pleas swallowed by the crowd's frantic movement.

"Open the gate!" a man near the front shouted, his fists pounding against the locked metal. "We have a right to survive!"

The soldiers at the gate stood firm, weapons drawn.

Their expressions were hard as they pushed back against the crowd, tension radiating from each one. Their mission was clear: to prevent anyone unapproved from entering. Their eyes scanned the crowd, noting each new surge forward and assessing the mounting danger.

"Back off!" one of the soldiers yelled, his hand poised on his weapon. "We're authorized to use force if necessary!"

The threat only seemed to inflame the crowd. Anger blazing in his eyes, another man pushed his way to the front. "You think the government cares about you? They're going to leave you out here to die, same as the rest of us! You're just pawns to them!"

One of the soldiers moved forward, taking the man firmly by the arm and pulling him aside. "I'm Private Stiles," he said in a low voice. "Look, man, I agree this situation's wrong. As soldiers, we took an oath to protect our citizens. This isn't a war against another nation—it's a battle against our government's lack of care."

Emily caught sight of the soldier speaking with the man, and something about their quiet conversation drew her over. She pushed her way through the crowd, straining to hear what they were saying.

"What's happening here?" she asked as she approached them.

The man turned toward her. "Who are you?"

"Just another concerned citizen," she replied. "I'm Emily."

The soldier gave her a slight nod. "I'm Jake. Look, Emily, we're all on the clock here. I will open the gate, but we'll need a distraction. I'm not letting everyone die out here if I can help it. Even if we make it inside, we may not survive—but at least it's a chance."

The man nodded, his jaw set. "Tell us what you need."

"I'll need you to cause a commotion and draw the other soldiers' attention," Jake replied. "I'll handle the gate controls."

Emily looked around at the anxious faces in the crowd. She turned back to the man. "Let's do this."

"It's all we've got," he agreed, his voice solemn.

Jake's expression turned determined. "The second the gate opens, you can't stop. Get through the bunker doors, and don't look back. It's going to be madness in there."

As they turned back toward the crowd, the man reached out to Emily. "I'm Frank. Nice to meet you."

"Nice to meet you too, Frank," she said, shaking his

hand.

Frank gestured over his shoulder. "That's my wife, Jane, and my daughter, Lily," he said. He turned to Jane. "This is Emily. She's going to help us create a distraction so one of the soldiers can open the gate."

A spark of hope flashed in Jane's eyes. "This is it. Our chance to survive."

Frank nodded, his gaze intense. "When the gate opens, hold on to Lily and don't let go. Keep running until you're inside the bunker."

"What about you?" Jane asked.

Frank placed a reassuring hand on her shoulder. "I'll be right behind you. Just focus on getting Lily to safety."

Emily and Frank moved down the fence from the gate, surveying the area as they thought through their plan.

"We need to make some noise, something big enough to get their attention," Frank muttered, his eyes darting around.

Emily considered their options. "We could start by shaking the fence. If enough people join in, it might be enough to draw them away from the gate."

Frank's eyes lit up. "Let's give it a try."

They grabbed the fence, rocking it repeatedly with

as much strength as possible. At first, it was only them, but others quickly caught on, and soon, the whole crowd joined, the collective force turning the fence into a pulsing, trembling barrier of desperation.

"Stop that!" a soldier shouted, racing toward the fence. "Get out of here, now!"

But the crowd only shook the fence harder, the rattle growing louder as they poured all their energy into breaking through. Hidden in the guard shack, Jake kept an eye on the unfolding chaos, knowing his moment was approaching fast.

With a deep breath, he moved to the control panel, his fingers hesitating only a second before pressing the button.

"The gate's opening!" someone yelled from the crowd, the shout igniting a new surge of energy. "Run, everyone! Run!"

Emily and Frank sprinted toward the opening with the crowd on their heels, driven forward by the overpowering urge to survive.

From his position, Jake watched the chaos spill into motion. He knew he was gambling everything on this decision but couldn't turn his back on these people. He only hoped they would all make it inside.

The crowd surged through the gate and rushed

toward the bunker doors, desperate for safety. Soldiers tried to hold them back, but the mass of people was unstoppable, pushing against the armed forces with relentless energy born of fear. Scuffles broke out, and suddenly, shots rang out, the sounds piercing the air as soldiers fired warning shots in an attempt to regain control. But the crowd kept moving forward.

As Frank raced through the gate, he found Jane and Lily already sprinting ahead, and he hurried to catch up, his heart pounding. Emily was close behind, her pulse racing as she pushed herself to keep up.

Inside the bunker, General Michaels received frantic reports from his men. "What's going on out there?" he barked into the intercom. "I need answers, now!"

A panicked voice crackled through the line. "Sir, the crowd is forcing their way inside! They're breaking through!"

"Seal the doors!" General Michaels ordered, his voice cold. "Don't let them in!"

But it was too late. The crowd had already reached the entrance and poured a flood of desperate humanity into the bunker.

Inside, the bunker's occupants froze in shock as people surged through. Some tried to resist, but they were quickly overpowered and shoved aside. Several guards attempted to push back at the crowd, but the sheer volume of people made any attempt at control impossible.

General Michaels arrived, only to be overrun himself, pushed back by the force. In the chaos, he was shoved into a room and locked in with other guards. Jake finally arrived and quickly ran to the control panel to shut the bunker doors.

As the chaos settled, David returned to the entrance hall, his gaze sharp as he took in the overwhelming sight of the crowd. Spotting Frank, he approached, his expression alarmed. "What's going on here? How did all these people get inside?"

Frank quickly explained the situation, and David's face contorted with anger as he realized his wife had not yet arrived. "Open the doors now! My wife is out there!"

Emily stepped forward, trying to calm David down. "You need to settle down, or you'll be locked up with the others," she said, her voice firm. "The doors are closed. They're staying closed."

David's rage melted into a hopeless despair as he processed the reality of the situation. "You probably just killed everyone in here by doing this. We're overcrowded."

Just as David began to walk away, a voice called out, "David!"

David spun around, disbelief spreading across his face as he saw his wife, Mary, running toward him. He caught her in a tight embrace. "Mary! How did you get here?"

Mary clung to him, tears streaming down her cheeks. "An agent came for me," she explained, her voice choked with emotion. "The crowd was rushing the bunker when we arrived. I managed to make it inside just before the doors closed."

David held her close. "I thought I'd lost you," he whispered.

* * *

An hour passed as the crowd lingered near the bunker's entrance, uncertainty hanging thick in the air. They had found shelter, but the impending strike left them all on edge. General Michaels remained confined, seething at the turn of events. Eventually, he accepted the grim reality of the overcrowded bunker. He pounded on the door until Frank came over to speak with him.

"Frank, listen to me," he said. "We must get

everyone down to the lower levels before the asteroids hit. The doors will hold, but we can't be up here when it happens."

Frank eyed him warily. "How can we trust you?"

Jake stepped forward. "I'll make sure he doesn't try anything stupid."

General Michaels took a deep breath. "There's no time left. We have to work together if we're going to have a chance at surviving the impact."

Emily joined them, catching the end of the conversation. "What's happening?" she asked.

"The General is telling us we need to get deeper underground," Frank explained. "Jake will be assisting him."

"Sounds like a good idea," Emily agreed. "Let's get moving. I'll gather everyone."

Emily addressed the group, her voice ringing through the crowded space. "Everyone, listen up. We need to move to the lower levels. Stay calm and move slowly. Let's keep this organized."

She turned back to General Michaels. "Lead the way, General."

The General nodded, calling out to the crowd, "This way, everyone. Follow me."

They headed to the elevators, and in small groups at

a time, they were lowered to the deepest level of the bunker. Once everyone was safely down there, General Michaels addressed Jake. "We need to brace for impact. Tell them to prepare."

Jake moved to the intercom, speaking firmly. "Everyone, listen up. We're preparing for impact. Line up against the walls, get down on your knees, and put your heads down. We need to be ready."

Fear settled over the crowd as they followed his instructions, each person huddling against the walls. Silence filled the air, punctuated only by soft sobs and murmured prayers.

Emily glanced at Jake. "Do you think we'll be okay?"

Jake's jaw clenched. "I don't know, Emily. I just don't know."

"How long do we have?" Frank asked the General.

Before the General could answer, a low rumble began to shake the floor. Everyone held their breath as the vibrations intensified, rolling through the bunker like waves. Then, a sudden, loud bang echoed through the chamber, and the ground shuddered beneath them. Panic broke out as the bunker rocked violently.

Suddenly, the shaking stopped as quickly as it had begun. The room fell silent, and the lights flickered before going out, plunging them into darkness.

Chapter 4

"Got it," Jake said confidently as he reached up and flipped the switch. After nearly twenty hours in darkness, the lights finally filled the rooms again.

Emily rubbed her eyes, adjusting to the brightness. "Impressive," she said with admiration. "Where'd you learn to do that?"

"I studied engineering during my time in the military," Jake replied. "I've always had a knack for fixing things."

"Well, I'm glad you were here to save the day," Emily said with a soft smile. "Let's head back up top."

"Remind me why you insisted on coming down here with me?" Jake asked, giving her a playful look.

"I didn't," Emily shot back with a grin. "You handed me the flashlight and told me to follow you."

"Right," Jake said with a chuckle. "It's been a long day."

"At least we can take the elevator back up instead of the stairs," Emily noted with a tired smile.

"So, what did you do before all this?" Jake asked as they stepped into the elevator.

"Oh, I wouldn't want to bore you," Emily replied.

Jake chuckled. "No, what is it?"

Emily smiled. "Alright, I was a public speaker for situational awareness."

"Ah…that makes sense," Jake said.

Emily stepped back and crossed her arms. "Oh, really?" she replied in a teasing tone.

"Yeah," Jake said. "You really stepped up out there. You assessed the situation and jumped into action. Then you did it again in here. You took control of the chaos and got people to calm down."

Emily smiled. "Well, I wouldn't say that I'm an expert at it," she said, "but I've been doing it long enough to get me out of certain situations." Her mind recalled a few late-night memories on the streets of the city. "It's a dangerous world out there."

"It sure is," Jake agreed.

The elevator doors slid open, and Emily spotted General Michaels, who was observing the scene with a watchful eye.

"What's the plan?" she asked as she approached him.

The General scanned the crowd. "Until we know what's happening up there, we need everyone settled in."

He turned, facing the crowd. His gaze swept across the group. "Before we get everyone settled, we need to do a headcount," he announced.

A low murmur of agreement rippled through the crowd as they organized to count off. When the headcount was complete, the final number came in at 223. General Michaels took a deep breath, his face revealing a flicker of concern.

"All right," he said, regaining his composure. "Let's head down to the second level, which will serve as our living quarters."

As they descended, General Michaels stopped at a map of the bunker and began outlining each level's function. "Let me explain the layout," he said.

"**Level 1:** Entrance—the top level where we just were.

Level 2: Living quarters—this is where we are now. The hallways are lined with rooms, but there are only 100, so you'll need to pair up.

Level 3: Food storage—all food supplies are here. Until further notice, nobody touches the food.

Level 4: Power generators—where we generate power for the entire bunker.

Level 5: Agriculture—we can grow food here if necessary, though hopefully, we won't be down here long enough to need it.

Level 6: Water filtration—where we purify our water supply.

Level 7: Waste management—this level handles waste disposal.

Level 8: Control room and communications— where we'll monitor radiation levels and try to establish outside contact.

Level 9: Medical facilities—where medical supplies are stored.

Level 10: Storage—holds everything we don't need immediately."

General Michaels looked around at the group as he concluded. "This is what we're working with. Let's get everyone settled in and make the best of this situation."

As people began finding rooms and getting situated, Frank approached Emily with a troubled look. "We need to keep an eye on the General," he said quietly.

"Why?" Emily asked, curious.

"People are talking," Frank explained. "He's taking control, and not everyone's thrilled. He's already restricted us from the food, and we've been here for a day. I don't know about everyone else, but I'm starving."

Emily nodded, understanding his concerns. "I get it. We're overcrowded and don't know how much food we have. But people can't go hungry. I'll talk to him and see if we can get something worked out."

A commotion erupted nearby, drawing their attention. General Michaels was berating a gathering crowd when they arrived at the scene.

"You people invaded my bunker!" he shouted, his voice ringing in the enclosed space. "Stay away from the elevators! Nobody is going anywhere until I say so!"

Emily stepped forward, her voice calm but firm. "What's happening here?"

A desperate voice rose from the crowd. "We need food! We won't just sit here following orders while we starve!"

Frustration simmered among the people, and the tension in the room grew thicker with each passing second.

Frank saw the situation deteriorating quickly. He addressed the crowd, "Everyone, please, let's keep this peaceful. Emily, talk to General Michaels—I'll help calm things down here."

As Emily turned toward the General, Jake stepped up beside her. "I'll stay here and help Frank," he offered.

"Thank you, Jake," Emily said, grateful for his support.

Emily approached the General, who was pacing tensely near the elevators. His agitation was evident, but she knew they needed to find a way to address the group's growing unease.

"General Michaels," she began gently, "I understand this is difficult, but we need to find a way to calm things down."

"Calm down?" he repeated, his voice sharp with frustration. "These people have no right to be here. They've overrun my bunker and put our resources at risk. How am I supposed to be calm?"

"I know it's a difficult situation," Emily replied, "but people here need your help. If we don't find a solution, this could end badly for everyone."

"We don't have enough resources for 200 people," he argued.

Emily held her ground. "I'm not an expert on bunkers, but we have enough for now. I understand things must be managed carefully, but the resources won't disappear in a day."

"That's not the point," he snapped. "The point is that these people shouldn't even be here. They're jeopardizing everything."

"I understand that," Emily said, calm but insistent. "But you must remember, everyone here is only trying to survive. They didn't come here by choice; they came out of necessity. Right now, people are hungry. They need food. Once we've addressed that, we can focus on how to manage things long-term."

The General sighed. "Fine," he conceded. "We'll distribute some food. But I want it clear—this isn't a permanent solution."

Emily nodded, relieved. "Thank you, General. I'll make sure the distribution is orderly."

As she returned to the crowd, Emily couldn't shake a sense of unease. This was only the beginning of what promised to be a long and arduous ordeal. General Michaels was volatile, and she suspected his patience would wear thin quickly. His temper and rigid adherence to protocol were concerning, and she feared that conflicts would continue.

Despite the challenges ahead, Emily remained vigilant. She was determined to protect the people here and create some semblance of order in the coming days. They must navigate the situation carefully to prevent more incidents, especially if the General's temper flared again.

As people started receiving their food portions, there was a palpable shift in mood. It was far from peaceful, but the immediate threat of unrest had been subdued. Emily took a moment to watch as everyone settled into their makeshift dining spaces, quietly eating and trying to regain a sense of normalcy.

One by one, people began retreating to their rooms.

Emily sat beside Frank, who looked relieved that the situation was handled so calmly.

"That could have gone south fast," he said quietly.

"I know," Emily agreed. "But at least we managed to get some food out. Hopefully, that'll hold everyone for now."

Frank glanced over at General Michaels, who was now speaking with a group of his soldiers. "He's not going to let this slide easily," he said. "We need to be prepared for him to crack down harder."

Emily sighed, "We'll cross that bridge when we come to it. We must stay alert and take it one step at a time."

Hours passed, and soon, the bunker was quiet. Most of the people had turned in for the night. Emily, however, lay awake, her thoughts heavy. She could feel the weight of her responsibility, and although she had no official role, she sensed that many people were already looking up to her.

* * *

The following day, Emily waited until General Michaels was alone before approaching him. He looked up, his expression wary as she approached.

"General," she began, her tone even, "I think we should discuss a long-term plan for managing resources and keeping morale up."

He sighed heavily, but she noticed a slight softening in his demeanor. "What do you propose?" he asked, not entirely dismissive.

Emily took a breath. "We could form a council. A few people for each section of the bunker—food, water, security, and medical. It could help manage resources and communicate the group's needs. It could take some pressure off you and help the others feel they have a voice."

General Michaels mulled it over. "You're suggesting a democratic process?" he asked, his tone skeptical.

"Not entirely," Emily clarified. "But if the people feel included, they're less likely to push back. We're all trapped here together, General. The more unified we are, the better our chances."

After a pause, he gave a slow nod. "I'll consider it," he said, though his tone remained guarded. "But understand, Emily, I won't tolerate any challenges to my authority. This bunker is still under military command."

"Understood," Emily replied, knowing it was the best compromise she would get. "Thank you for considering it."

As she walked away, she allowed herself a small glimmer of hope. If the General agreed with the council, they might have a chance of maintaining order. The challenges were far from over, but they might survive with cooperation and careful planning. It was a fragile peace for now but something to build on.

Chapter 5

"Put the gun down, General!" Frank shouted, his hands raised as the cold barrel pressed against his temple.

Chaos filled the room as the survivors scrambled to defuse the tension. Some ran back to their rooms, while others tried to reason with the General. Only a week had passed since the impact, and the tension between the General and the people had reached a boiling point. Emily watched in horror, and Jake came up beside her.

"I thought we secured all the weapons before letting everyone roam freely in the bunker," she said.

Regret began to fill Jake's eyes. "I thought I got

them all," he replied, "but he must have had a one hidden somewhere."

"This is my bunker, and everyone will follow my orders!" the General shouted, his face flushed with fury. "You should never have challenged me, Frank! Look where you are now."

Frank remained steady. "Please, calm down," he said. "Nobody needs to get hurt here. We all want peace."

Emily stepped forward, her voice carrying through the tension-filled room. "This isn't leadership, General. This is not how you guide people. No one will trust you if you keep acting like this."

While she spoke, Jake moved carefully along the edge of the crowd, his focus fixed on the gun.

"This is my bunker under my orders!" The general yelled again. "I won't have any of you do anything here without my permission."

"We are all human beings here," Emily said. "This isn't a military bunker anymore, General. This is our survival. Put the gun down now!"

As the General slowly lowered the gun, Jake seized his moment. He lunged, tackling the General to the ground. Frank quickly joined him, struggling to wrestle the gun away. Grunts and cries filled the air as the three fought for control. Suddenly, a gunshot rang out, echoing throughout the room. People screamed, backing away in fear, hands instinctively covering their heads.

Emily rushed over to the three men lying on the floor, her heart pounding. "Is everyone okay?" she asked, her voice trembling. "Did anyone get hurt?"

Frank stood up, and Jake rolled over, revealing the General lying motionless on the floor, a bullet wound in his chest.

"We need help!" Emily cried out, desperation filling her tone. "Sarah! Where are you?"

Dr. Sarah ran over, and together, they rushed the General to the medical level, where they began efforts to revive him.

Working quickly, Sarah took command. "We need to get his heart rate back up," she directed. "Emily, start chest compressions. Frank, go get the defibrillator."

The three moved with urgency, trying to bring the General back. Emily counted compressions while Frank readied the defibrillator.

Sarah prepared the paddles. "Clear!" she called, pressing the paddles to the General's chest. His body jerked, but he showed no signs of life.

"Again!" Sarah instructed, and they repeated the

process, but there was still no response. "Emily, go get the IV line."

As Emily prepared the IV, their efforts remained futile. The General's body lay unresponsive.

"Again!" Sarah said, her determination strong. "Clear!" she called, pressing the paddles once more. But it was too late—the General was dead.

Emily felt a deep sadness settle in as she looked at Frank. "I never thought it would end like this," she said, her voice breaking as tears began to fall.

"What happened here?" Sarah asked, her tone filled with confusion.

"The General was trying to enforce a curfew," Frank explained. "He was ordering everyone to stay in their rooms, refusing to let them move freely. I tried reasoning with him, but he wouldn't listen. He just pulled out the gun."

Emily shook her head. "You couldn't have known he had the gun, Frank."

Frank sighed, the weight of the incident heavy on him. "I know, but I don't understand how I threatened him. I was only trying to offer a solution."

"Don't dwell on it," Emily said softly. "I'm going to check on Jake."

Emily stepped out and spotted Jake standing nearby,

visibly shaken. She approached, her voice gentle, "Jake, are you okay?"

Jake nodded, then hesitated. "I…I'm not sure," he admitted, his voice trembling. "I tried to turn the gun away, but he must've kept his finger on the trigger. It went off, and…he shot himself."

Emily placed a reassuring hand on Jake's shoulder. "It's not your fault, Jake. The General's behavior was irrational, and this was a tragic accident. You did what you could to protect everyone—that's all anyone could ask of you."

Jake looked at her, his eyes filled with gratitude. "Thank you, Emily. I keep replaying that moment, thinking I should have done more. But you're right; I did what I could in the situation."

Emily nodded with a warm smile. "We all make mistakes and have regrets, but what matters is that we learn from them and keep going. Right now, take some time to process everything. I'm here if you need anything."

Jake returned her smile, "Thank you, Emily."

"Come on," she said, "let's inform the others."

Emily went to the General's office, the weight of recent events pressing down on her. She took a deep breath, pressed the button on the intercom, and called for everyone to a meeting.

As the residents gathered, Emily took a deep breath and spoke, "Everyone, I have an important announcement to make."

The room fell silent as she shared the news of General Michaels's death.

From the crowd, a voice cried out, "What? How could this happen?"

Another voice said, "He was strict but kept us safe."

Murmurs of agreement spread.

Then, unexpectedly, another voice spoke up, "Good riddance. He never made decisions that benefited the group."

Emily's voice cut through the air. "Stop! This is not something to celebrate. General Michaels may not have been the leader we hoped for, but wishing harm on someone in a situation like this is unacceptable. We're all down here together and need unity, not division."

Frank stepped forward, "Emily's right. If we're going to survive, we need a steady leader."

A voice from the crowd called out, "So you're saying you want to be our leader, Frank?"

Frank shook his head. "No, I don't want that role," he replied. He turned to Emily. "I think Emily should lead. She's been a voice of reason from the start.

Without her, we wouldn't have made it here. Remember, she was the first to lead the way, distracting the soldiers while Jake opened the gate."

The crowd began to murmur, and then Jake stepped forward. "I second the motion to have Emily as our leader."

One by one, people nodded and voiced their agreement.

Emily looked at Frank, her voice wavering, "Are you sure I'm the right person for this?"

Frank put a hand on her shoulder. "I'm certain. You'll do great. This bunker needs strong leadership, and you're the best person for the job."

Taking a deep breath, Emily nodded, feeling the weight of responsibility settle on her.

As the meeting drew to a close, she heard one last voice speak up. "We believe in you, Emily."

The crowd dispersed, leaving her standing alone with her thoughts. She took a deep breath, whispering, "I won't let you down."

Chapter 6

"David, what's the update on the radiation levels?" Emily asked as she entered the control room.

David turned to her, his face serious. "It's not good. The levels keep climbing."

Emily sighed, leaning against the control panel. "We've been down here six months now. How much longer before the levels peak and start going down?"

David shook his head. "I don't know, but however long it is, it's enough to keep us down here for a while."

Just then, Jake entered the room. "Any good news?" he asked, a note of hope in his voice.

Emily shook her head. "No, just more bad news." She turned to Jake. "What about you? Any luck with communications? Have you made contact with other bunkers?"

Jake sighed, "Nothing yet. Still trying."

Emily patted David's shoulder. "Keep watching those levels, and let me know if there's any change."

"Will do," David replied.

"I'm going to check in with Frank," Emily said. "I need to see how he's doing with his rounds."

* * *

Frank was heading back to the kitchen to grab another cup of coffee when he was stopped by a bunker resident.

"Frank," a woman called quietly, glancing around to ensure they weren't overheard.

"Yes, ma'am," Frank replied, noticing her nervous expression. "Is something wrong?"

She leaned in, whispering. "I don't want anyone to know I told you this, but I think someone's been stealing food from storage."

Frank frowned. "Why do you think that?"

"Well," she said hesitantly, "I was on my way to the

Rec Room and noticed one of the resident's door was opened. I peeked in to see if anyone was inside and saw boxes of food under the bed. It wasn't the usual rations. There were several of them."

Frank sighed. He had known that with close quarters and limited supplies, tensions could drive people to desperate actions. "What room was it?" he asked.

"Room 87," she replied, glancing over her shoulder. "Please don't tell anyone I told you."

"Don't worry," Frank assured her. "I'll say I found it on my own. Cop's honor." He smiled, hoping to put her at ease.

Frank made his way to Room 87 and knocked. When no one answered, he opened the door and stepped inside. Sure enough, several boxes of food were stacked under the bed. Frank shook his head, disappointment settling in.

Just then, a young man in his late teens stepped in. "Can I help you with something?" he asked, surprised to see Frank in his room.

"Is this your room, Jared?" Frank asked, keeping his tone steady. "I need to talk to you about these boxes under your bed."

Jared's face drained of color. "That food is mine,"

he said defensively. "I was just saving it for a rainy day."

"Jared," Frank replied sternly, "that's not how things work here. We agreed to share resources equally and conserve our supplies. Taking food from storage is against everything we're trying to uphold as a community."

Jared looked down, clearly embarrassed. "I'm sorry," he mumbled. "I didn't think it would be a big deal. There's plenty of food stocked up."

Frank shook his head. "That's no excuse, Jared. We're all in this together. I'll have to take this food back to storage."

Jared nodded, looking defeated. "I understand. It won't happen again. Maybe I wouldn't have been so worried if the gardens were up and running."

Frank nodded thoughtfully. "I'll bring it up with Emily," he said, gathering the boxes.

On his way to storage, he ran into Emily in the elevator.

"Frank," Emily said, looking relieved. "I was just looking for you. How's everything going on your end?"

"It's going alright," Frank replied. "But I just dealt with a little situation."

Emily's eyes moved to the boxes of food Frank was

carrying. "What happened?"

Frank sighed. "You know that troubled teen Jared?" Emily shook her head, clearly understanding what Frank was talking about. "I can't believe he'd do that. Taking food like that is against everything we're trying to build here."

"Don't worry, I talked with him," Frank assured her. "He understood the importance of working together. I don't think he'll do it again."

Emily nodded, a hint of relief in her expression. "I'm glad to hear that. I'm grateful we have someone like you to keep things in order. You make sure everyone's held accountable."

Frank gave her a smile. "I'm just doing my job, ma'am. I want everyone to feel safe and secure down here."

"Well, you're doing a great job," Emily said, patting him on the shoulder. "Keep it up."

"Thanks, Emily," Frank replied. "Oh, by the way, Jared mentioned something."

"What's that?" Emily asked.

"He brought up the gardens," Frank said. "Are there any plans to get them started?"

Emily chuckled. "Funny you should mention that. I just spoke with Robert, our agriculturalist. He's been preparing the equipment, and we hope to start planting next week."

Frank smiled. "So, the gardens are finally in the works?"

"Yes," Emily confirmed. "Robert's setting things up. The gardens weren't operational when we arrived, and most of the equipment was still in storage. But with the uncertainty of how long we'll be here, it's time to get them going."

"That's great to hear," Frank said, visibly relieved. "With no end in sight, having fresh food will be essential."

"It sure will," Emily agreed.

"You know," Frank said thoughtfully, "I've noticed that people appreciate having the Rec Room. I never would have guessed a bunker like this would have space for entertainment."

Emily laughed. "Government officials need their downtime, too."

Frank chuckled. "I guess so. Though it doesn't seem like they were doing much of anything useful anyway."

They shared a laugh before saying their goodbyes, each heading off to continue the rest of their day.

Chapter 7

"Robert, I heard you're having trouble with the gardens," Emily said as she arrived to the agricultural level.

"Yes," Robert replied. "The air vents haven't been installed yet. They're still packed away in storage."

Emily let out a sigh. "We picked the wrong bunker to weather this out." She grabbed the radio at her side. "Jake, are you there?"

"What's up?" Jake's voice crackled through. "Everything okay?"

"Everything's fine," Emily assured him. "Just need you to stop by the gardens if you can."

"On my way," Jake replied.

Emily turned back to Robert. "We'll get it fixed. In the meantime, we still have a good stock of food."

Robert smiled, nodding. "I know, Emily. I just want to get the gardens running smoothly. We've been down here for nine months now, and the last two have been spent getting everything prepped and planted. It's been a challenge."

Just then, Jake entered the room. "What's going on?" he asked.

"Robert's having trouble with the garden's," Emily explained. "We need the vents from storage installed as soon as possible."

"Got it," Jake said. "I'll get it taken care of as soon as I'm finished with my rounds."

"Thanks, Jake," Emily said. "I know it's another task on your list, but I appreciate it."

"No problem," Jake replied with a smile.

"Thank you both for your help," Robert added. "I appreciate the effort."

"We're glad to lend a hand," Emily replied.

* * *

Jake was on his way to check the generators when

he spotted Frank's daughter, Lily, walking down the hall.

"Hey, Lily, have you seen your dad?" Jake asked.

"I think he's with Dr. Sarah in the medical facility," Lily replied.

"Is he okay?" Jake asked, a touch of concern in his voice.

"He's been having headaches," Lily said. "Dr. Sarah's trying to figure out what's causing them."

"Thanks for the update, Lily," Jake said. "Tell him I'm looking for him if you see him before I do."

"I will," Lily promised.

"By the way," Jake added with a smile, "how are you holding up here?"

Lily sighed. "It's boring sometimes. But there are movies in the Rec Room."

Jake smiled. "Maybe we'll have a movie night sometime. It's been a while since I'v watched one."

Lily's face lit up. "That sounds fun! You can even pick the movie."

"Sounds like a plan," Jake replied. "Take care, Lily."

"Bye, Jake" Lily said as she turned and skipped away down the hall.

* * *

Frank and his wife, Jane, were seated in Dr. Sarah's office, waiting for her arrival.

"I hope Sarah can figure out what's causing your headaches," Jane said, concern lacing her voice.

"I'm sure it's nothing," Frank reassured her.

Jane leaned over, kissing his cheek. "I hope you're right."

Moments later, Sarah entered, looking apologetic. "Sorry for the delay. Another patient wasn't feeling well. Adjusting to bunker food hasn't been easy for anyone."

Jane wrinkled her nose. "I can't stand the food here. I wish we had something fresh."

Sarah nodded in agreement. "We all do." She turned to Frank. "So, Frank, how are you feeling today?"

Frank shook his head. "Ever since we arrived in the bunker, I've been getting these headaches."

Sarah studied him closely, noting the fatigue in his eyes. "Are you getting enough sleep?"

"Not really," Frank said. "It's overwhelming being the one responsible for keeping peace here. Sometimes, I wish I could just lock the troublemakers up and not have to worry about them."

Jane laughed lightly, "He's just kidding."

Sarah smiled. "Have you thought about recruiting some help?" she suggested.

Frank paused, considering. Before the bunker, he'd been a cop with backup and support. Since arriving, he'd handled all the patrolling and conflict resolution himself.

"That's a good idea," he said thoughtfully.

Sarah walked over to a cabinet and took out a small medication box. "Here," she said, handing it to Frank. "Take these to help you sleep. If you find some help with the work, the headaches should ease up, too."

"Thanks, Doc," Frank said gratefully.

* * *

"Good, good, and good," Jake murmured to himself, checking off the final items on his list. Satisfied that the generators were in top shape, he walked toward the elevator. As he passed, he glanced at a large wooden box tucked in the corner—the makeshift resting place of General Michaels. The bunker had no morgue so they'd found an airtight container to store his body. Jake shook his head and stepped into the elevator.

When he arrived on the medical level, he spotted

Frank and Jane leaving Sarah's office.

"Hey, Frank," Jake greeted him. "Lily said you'd be here. Is everything alright?"

Frank nodded. "Yeah, just need more sleep and maybe a bit less stress."

Jane nudged him playfully. "Don't forget to hire some rookies, Chief."

Frank laughed, "Yes, I'll get on it."

Jake smiled. "I know a couple of guys who might be interested. I'll send them your way."

"Thanks, Jake," Frank replied appreciatively.

"No problem," Jake said. "By the way, did you mention a troubled kid in here before?"

Frank thought for a moment. "Yeah, his name's Jared. I caught him hoarding food a while back. He's young—just out of high school."

Jake nodded. "I need some help with a job Emily gave me. Do you know where I can find him?"

"Probably in the Rec Room," Frank replied. "He spends a lot of time there."

"Thanks," Jake said. "I hope you feel better soon." He smiled at Jane. "Good to see you again."

"It's good to see you, too, Jake," Jane replied. "Thanks for all you do."

"You're welcome," Jake said. "Take care."

* * *

Jared was sorting through some music albums in the Rec Room when Jake found him. The room had everything from movies to board games and even a collection of puzzles.

"Hey, Jared," Jake greeted him. "I need a hand with something."

"Sure, what is it?" Jared asked, putting the album down.

"Robert's having a hard time with the gardens," Jake explained. "We need some vents installed to improve airflow. Think you can help?"

Jared's face brightened. "I'd love to! I've been looking forward to fresh food."

"Great," Jake said. "Let's grab the vents from storage."

As they made their way to storage, Jake asked, "So, what did you do before…all this?"

"I played a lot of football," Jared said. "I was going to try for a college team."

"I used to play, too," Jake said, smiling at the memory. "Even played with the other soldiers when we had downtime. It was a good way to keep fit."

"At least you got to keep playing," Jared said

67

wistfully.

"Yeah," Jake replied. "Good memories."

They stepped off the elevators on the storage level and began looking for the boxes with the vents.

"Do you have a favorite football team?" Jake asked.

"I'm a Packers fan," Jared replied.

Jake laughed. "I'm more of a Patriots guy."

"That's tough competition," Jared joked. "I always loved watching them play."

"Same here," Jake agreed. "The Patriots had this way of coming together and pulling off wins when it mattered."

Jared nodded. "And the Packers always had a strong defense."

"Imagine if we could watch another game," Jake said. "It might not happen again in our lifetime."

"That would be a shame," Jared replied, a hint of sadness in his voice.

* * *

Frank returned to his room after a long day. He took the medication Sarah had given him, hoping for some relief from his lingering headache. Just as he was about to lie down, there was a knock on the door. He opened it, expecting another bunker issue. Instead, two young men stood there, eager to speak.

"Hey, Frank," one said. "Jake sent us over. I'm Daniel."

"And I'm Rob," the other introduced himself.

Frank shook their hands. "Nice to meet you both. That was quick."

"Jake caught us on his way to storage," Daniel explained. "Said you might need help."

"Yeah, I could use it," Frank admitted. "Most days are calm, but handling it alone can get exhausting when conflicts break out."

"We get that," Rob said. "So, what do you need from us?"

Frank considered. "Just help keep peace and resolve issues among the residents. I'll let everyone know you're here to help."

"Sounds good," Daniel replied, nodding.

"There's no pay down here," Frank joked.

Rob shrugged. "Just having peace is enough for us."

Frank chuckled. "Glad to hear it. I'm grateful you both are willing to help."

Daniel nodded. "Happy to be on board."

* * *

Robert continued tending to the plants in the gardens when he heard a pallet jack rolling into the room. He looked up from his garden to see Jake and Jared approaching him.

"Hey, guys," Robert greeted them with a tired but hopeful smile. "Are those the vents?"

"Yep," Jared replied, grinning.

"Thank goodness," Robert said with relief. "The plants have been struggling without proper ventilation."

Jake surveyed the room. "Do you know how these are supposed to be installed?"

Robert pointed to the wall where several panels were mounted. "The main system was partially installed outside the garden room, but these panels need to be removed to connect the vents. The vents will run along the ceiling above the garden. I found a set of blueprints that should help."

Jake took the blueprints, studying them carefully. "Looks manageable. Let's get started."

They began removing the panels from the wall, exposing the openings where the vents would be installed. As they worked, Emily entered the room, curious about their progress.

"How's it going, guys?" she asked, smiling as she looked around the place.

"We just got started on the vents," Jake said, wiping some dust from his hands. "Everything okay on your end?"

"I just wanted to check in," Emily replied. She turned to Robert. "I'd love to learn more about how this setup works."

Robert's face lit up. "It's a bit of a mix here," he explained. "These plants are growing hydroponically—their roots are in water, not soil, which lets us control nutrients more precisely. And these over here," he gestured to rows of leafy greens, "these are in soil but need proper aeration to grow well."

Emily listened intently, impressed by the complexity. "I didn't realize how detailed this was. You've been doing an incredible job, Robert."

Robert beamed, clearly proud. "Thank you, Emily. I'm eager to get the airflow going so these plants can thrive."

Jake, holding up a vent, turned to Jared. "Alright, let's get this first one set up. I'll help guide it in, and you can attach it with these bolts."

They worked as a team, installing one vent after another. Robert walked over occasionally to adjust the setup, ensuring the vents were positioned correctly. As they progressed, the room slowly began to fill with fresh air, circulating in a way that was already more comfortable for everyone inside.

Once the last vent was installed, Robert took a deep breath. "That's a huge improvement. You can feel the air moving now!"

"Feels better in here already," Jared added, stretching his arms as he breathed in the fresh air.

Emily looked around, nodding approvingly. "This will make a world of difference for the plants and us. Fresh produce could change everything down here."

"Couldn't have done it without you guys," Robert said sincerely.

"Glad to help," Jake replied. "And I think we earned a well-deserved break. How about we get some dinner?"

"Sounds good to me," Jared agreed.

Emily turned to Robert, "Thank you, Robert. I know this has been a long time, but you've brought this project to life."

Robert gave her a grateful nod. "Couldn't have done it without everyone's support."

As they left the garden room, Emily couldn't help but feel a renewed sense of hope.

Chapter 8

"Hello? Anybody there?"

Jake was jolted awake, the voice pulling him abruptly from his sleep. His surroundings blurred as he rubbed his eyes, scanning the quiet, dimly lit room, realizing with a start that the sound wasn't just part of a fading dream.

"Hello? Is anybody there?" the voice repeated, a bit louder this time, and Jake felt his mind snap fully into focus. Someone was trying to make contact on the radio.

Jake shot up, the urgency of the voice sharpening

his instincts. The radio had sat in silence for a year, only ever broadcasting the occasional static or, more recently, emitting faint mechanical beeps when its connection faded. Contact was nearly impossible in this radioactive silence they'd come to accept as their reality. Whoever was out there had managed to break through.

He pressed the button on the radio receiver, his heart hammering in his chest. "Hello! I'm here. This is Jake. Who is this?"

The radio crackled as if struggling to carry the sound across what must have been a vast distance, and then silence stretched, making Jake wonder if he'd already lost them. He waited, holding his breath, and then, with a faint hum, the voice returned.

"Thank God you're there," it said. "I've been calling for days now. My name is Tom. I…" the voice broke with a shuddering sigh "I need your help."

Jake's pulse quickened. This was the first time they'd contacted anyone outside the bunker. It was the first sign of life he had heard beyond their small circle of survivors. It felt unreal, like he was somehow imagining it.

"What kind of help do you need, Tom?" Jake asked, keeping his tone steady.

"We're in a private shelter beneath my house," Tom explained. His voice trembled, a mixture of exhaustion and desperation carrying through the static. "I've got my family here—my wife, my son. We've been down here since before the asteroids hit. We don't know what it's like outside and are scared to leave. We have no idea if it's even safe."

Jake felt the weight of Tom's words. He knew all too well the level of risk involved. He inhaled, steeling himself before responding. "I won't sugarcoat it, Tom. Conditions aren't great. Radiation levels are still dangerously high." He paused, imagining the bleak landscape above, knowing the exposure risks they would face if they ventured out now.

"How do you know that?" Tom asked.

Jake chose his words carefully. "We've…got ways to monitor the levels from down here. I can tell you, for your safety, you're better off where you are."

Tom was silent, and Jake imagined grim thoughts were swirling through his mind. When Tom finally spoke, his voice was barely above a whisper, "That's the problem. We're running low on supplies. We never thought we'd be down here for so long. We didn't stock it for more than a year. We tried to ration, but it's running out faster than expected."

Jake felt a chill, realizing the dilemma Tom and his family faced. The thought of leaving a family to starve, alone, in a place so close yet so unreachable twisted his gut.

"I can't make any promises," he said slowly. "But I'll see what we can do from here."

Tom exhaled in relief, and his voice softened with what sounded like tears of gratitude. "Just hearing someone else is out there…that alone is enough, Jake. You've given me hope."

"Hang in there," Jake replied, the heaviness of the conversation settling over him. He knew he'd have to talk to Emily about this, and there was no doubt it would be difficult. The risks of venturing beyond the bunker were extreme.

* * *

In the control room, David was bent over a set of monitors, poring over the latest data on radiation levels. His brow furrowed as he traced the graphs that, while remaining steady, showed a very gradual incline over the months.

"Still holding good?" Emily asked as she entered the room, glancing at the screens.

David looked up, his eyes tired but alert. "It seems like it, but…" he hesitated. "There's still an increase, subtle but there. The levels are still climbing."

"At least it's slowing down," Emily said, a sliver of hope in her voice. "Maybe things are finally starting to improve out there."

David exhaled, his tone guarded. "Maybe. But we can't know for certain. We can't stay down here forever, Emily. At some point, we'll need a way out."

Before Emily could respond, Jake entered, his expression urgent. "Emily, I need to talk to you."

"What's going on, Jake?" she asked, sensing something was off.

Jake wasted no time, his words tumbling out in a rush. "I received a radio transmission. Someone's out there."

Emily's eyes widened. "Who is it? Another government bunker?"

Jake shook his head. "No, it's a man named Tom. He and his family are housed in a private shelter under their house."

David, listening closely, seemed equally stunned. "You mean…civilians? Out there, surviving?"

Jake nodded. "They've been sheltered since the asteroids hit. But now they're almost out of supplies and need help. He reached out because he doesn't have many options left."

Emily's initial relief quickly dimmed, replaced by a concerned frown. "That's a terrible situation," she said, her voice heavy. "If they're that low on supplies…but what can we do? We can't jeopardize the safety of everyone here."

Jake's jaw tightened as he nodded. "I know. But we also can't ignore them. That's why I came to you first."

David spoke up, his voice laced with caution. "Look, we've talked about this. We can't open those doors. The radiation levels are too high. It's not safe."

Jake held up a hand. "I'm not saying we open the main doors. There is another way I didn't mention before. It was never needed until now."

Emily looked at him, intrigued. "Are you saying there's another way out?"

Jake glanced between them, then explained. "On level 7, waste management, there's an alternate access point—a hidden door that leads to a service tunnel. I blocked the door with some boxes of equipment so nobody finds it. The tunnel leads to an elevator that goes up to a secret level with a decontamination room and radiation suits."

Emily looked astonished. "How did you not

mention this?"

Jake shrugged sheepishly. "Would you have wanted them to know there was a way out on day one? Imagine if someone had tried to leave without knowing what was out there."

Emily laughed despite the gravity of the situation. "Fair point. If word got out, I could see people desperately trying it."

"That's why I didn't say anything," Jake admitted. "I thought it was safer if no one knew."

Emily nodded, the memory of the food hoarding incident with Jared flashing across her mind. She knew desperation could make anyone do anything. "So, are you suggesting that you want to go out there?"

Jake's voice was steady. "I know the decontamination procedures, and I can get to them. But I'm not an expert on radiation. I'd need someone to help me monitor the levels out there and ensure we don't expose ourselves beyond what the suits can handle."

David's face grew pale. "No, absolutely not. I can't do it. I'll show you how to read the levels, but there's no way I'm going out there."

Jake's gaze turned back to Emily, his expression grave. "You're the one in charge, Em. It's your call."

Emily's brow knitted, considering the lives they could potentially save while recognizing the life-threatening danger they'd face if they did. She finally asked, "How much time do they have?"

Jake's answer was solemn. "About three weeks of food left."

Emily swallowed, feeling the weight of her decision pressing down on her. She looked at David, his anxious gaze mirroring her own.

David cleared his throat. "Emily, I understand wanting to help them, but is it worth risking Jake's life? Or worse, the lives of everyone in the bunker?"

Jake interrupted gently, "I wouldn't go into this without being prepared. If we take precautions, the risk can be managed."

Emily's face softened as she took a deep breath. "Are you up for this, Jake? You'd be risking a lot for yourself."

Jake's eyes met hers. "If you give the word, I'm ready. I'll talk to Tom some more before making my final decision, but I believe it's worth a shot."

"If you do this," Emily replied, "just make sure you take care of yourself and stay out of trouble."

Jake nodded. "Don't worry, Emily. I'm sure I'll be ok."

* * *

Frank sat in the kitchen, savoring his coffee. The past few months had been significantly easier since Daniel and Rob had joined his efforts to maintain peace in the bunker. His headaches, once a constant companion, were practically nonexistent now. As he took another sip, he saw Jake entering the kitchen.

"Hey Frank, how's it going?" Jake asked, grabbing a coffee mug and joining him.

Frank smiled. "Doing alright, Jake. Thanks for checking. And thank you for spending time with Lily on her birthday. Watching that movie meant a lot to her."

Jake chuckled. "Lily's a wonderful kid. Tough, too, for sticking it out down here."

Frank's grin widened, a hint of excitement lighting up his eyes. "She won't be the youngest for long."

Jake blinked in surprise. "Wait—are you saying…?"

Frank nodded, his proud smile widening. "Yep. Jane and I just found out—she's three months along."

Jake's face broke into a huge smile, giving Frank a hearty clap on the back. "Congratulations, man! That's wonderful news."

"Thanks, but keep it quiet for now," Frank said, his expression softening. "Right now, just you, me, and

Sarah know."

"My lips are sealed," Jake promised as he poured himself some coffee. After a pause, he glanced at Frank. "I might have a big job coming up, Frank. One I need you to know about."

Frank's brow creased. "What's going on?"

Jake took a sip, setting the mug down. "I made contact with someone outside the bunker."

Frank's eyes widened, leaning in closer. "More survivors?"

"Yeah. His name's Tom," Jake explained. "He's with his wife and son. They're in a shelter under their house and almost out of supplies. I got the green light from Emily to go up and help them."

Frank looked confused. "But...how will you get out of here without exposing all of us?"

Jake continued on to explain the tunnel, the decontamination room, and the radiation suits. When he finished, Frank let out a low whistle. "That's a dangerous mission, Jake. I hope you're sure about this."

Jake nodded. "I am. We can't just let them starve out there if we have the ability to help them."

"When do you plan on heading out?" Frank asked, sounding cautious.

"Tomorrow morning," Jake replied. "David's been

showing me how to monitor radiation levels on a handheld device. I think I'm ready."

Frank finished his coffee, placing the cup down. "Then good luck, Jake. I'll be keeping you in my prayers."

"Thanks, Frank. I'll be doing a lot of praying myself," Jake replied with a smirk, though his voice carried a tinge of worry.

* * *

The following day, Emily woke with an unshakable sense of unease. Her first thought was of Jake. She'd tried to prepare herself, but the idea of him stepping out of the bunker alone into a world unknown filled her with dread. She forced herself to focus, taking a deep breath and telling herself he'd be fine.

After dressing, she stepped into the hallway, spotting Robert on his way to the gardens.

"Morning, Robert," she called, managing a small smile.

"Good morning, Emily," Robert replied, his face lighting up. "Those vents made all the difference. The plants are flourishing."

"Glad to hear it," she said. "We could use some

good news."

When Emily reached the control room, she found Jake already waiting. David gave him last-minute instructions, carefully explaining how to read the handheld radiation device.

"Are you sure about this?" Emily asked quietly, her heart pounding.

Jake turned to her, smiling softly. "As sure as I'll ever be. Don't worry about me, Em. I'll be fine."

She nodded, still nervous. "When should I tell everyone that new people might join us?"

Jake gave her a steady look. "After I've checked things out. They'll worry about contamination, but we need their support for this to work."

Emily sighed. "You're right. And with you and Frank backing me, I think it'll go over better."

Jake nodded, placing a comforting hand on her shoulder. "You've got this. Just keep things running here."

"Thank you, Jake," Emily replied. "I'll come with you down there and see you off."

Jake led Emily to level 7, clearing away the stacked boxes that were blocking the hidden door. Emily tried to steel herself, bracing for what was to come.

"This door here," Jake said, pointing, "leads to the

tunnel that goes to the elevator."

Together, they entered the tunnel, the dim lighting casting long shadows as they moved down the corridor. Emily felt her pulse quicken with each step. The air was thick with tension, her nerves on edge as the realization of Jake's mission settled over her.

At the tunnel's end, they reached the elevator. Jake pressed the button, and the doors slid open, revealing the small chamber. He turned to Emily, his face calm.

"This elevator leads to the decontamination room," he explained, his voice steady. "On the other side of that room, there's a ladder to the surface."

They stood in silence as the elevator took them up to their destination. As the elevator came to a stop and the doors opened, Emily nodded, the gravity of the moment sinking in. "So this is it."

They stepped out of the elevator, and Jake suited up in silence, methodically securing the gear with practiced hands. He packed three more suits for Tom and his family before slinging the bag over his shoulder. Emily watched him in awe. She'd always respected Jake's courage, but this felt different—far more personal and dangerous than any task he'd taken on before.

When he was ready, he gave her a reassuring nod. "Remember, I'll check in on the radio in a few hours."

Emily felt her throat tighten. "Stay safe out there, Jake."

He offered a smile before stepping into the decontamination chamber, the door sealing behind him with a soft hiss.

Chapter 9

Jake's eyes traced the outline of the metal ladder leading up to the hatch; each rung layered thickly with dust. The ladder looked fragile, almost ready to snap under his weight. He steadied himself, taking a deep breath to calm his racing heart, and began the climb. Each rung creaked and groaned, the ladder swaying slightly as he ascended, filling him with an acute awareness of his vulnerability. He was rising into an unknown world—a world he could only imagine after so long underground.

As he climbed, memories surfaced, pulling him briefly from the present moment. Scenes from his life before the asteroids hit drifted through his mind. The moments spent with family, laughter shared with friends, and the warmth of his home. He felt a pang of loss, recognizing a life he'd left behind, most likely forever. But despite the longing these memories stirred, he kept moving upward, knowing there was no turning back. He had promised Tom he would come, and that promise anchored him. Whatever awaited him at the top, he had to believe there was hope that life could persist despite the catastrophic destruction.

At last, he reached the top, his gloves brushing against the cool metal of the hatch. He twisted the handwheel, feeling the lock click open. Taking one final deep breath, he pushed the hatch upward, and a sudden, blinding light met his eyes. As his vision adjusted, he stepped out into the new world—a world transformed into barren desolation. The impact had turned the landscape into a vast wasteland. The earth lay lifeless, the trees reduced to brittle skeletons of the life that had once flourished here.

He shut the hatch door and lifted the steel panel that concealed the keypad. Entering the lock code, he heard a soft click as the hatch sealed shut, leaving him with a profound sense of isolation in this desolate, ravaged world.

Jake made his way toward the parking lot, his eyes scanning the area for any signs of life, though he saw only devastation. Cars lay mangled and crumpled, their frames twisted by the force of the blast. Tires had melted into the concrete, fusing them permanently to the ground. Shards of glass littered the asphalt, glittering faintly in the muted light.

"No one could have survived this out here," he muttered. The thought of those who hadn't reached safety churned his stomach. He could almost picture the scene at the bunker's entrance during those last moments—the rush of people, desperate for shelter, only to be turned away or left behind in the chaos. Not everyone had made it in, and he shuddered, trying not to dwell on the grim details.

But he couldn't allow himself to get lost in that memory now. He was out here for a reason—to help Tom and his family. He glanced at the radiation monitor in his hand, watching the red numbers blink ominously. They confirmed what he had feared: the radiation levels were still dangerously high. He had clung to a faint hope that maybe the control room's readings had been wrong, that perhaps he'd find a safer environment on the surface. But there was no denying the numbers. The levels were deadly, and there was no telling if it would ever be safe again.

Taking another steadying breath, he forced himself to keep moving, each step feeling heavy as if trudging through thick mud. Yet he continued forward, feeling the weight of his promise. He wasn't about to turn back.

His thoughts drifted to those he'd left behind in the bunker, the people he cared about. They were safe for now, but safety was fragile. He could only hope they would have the chance to walk outside without fear someday.

His boots crunched over rubble, and debris scattered across the pavement. The buildings around him barely stood; their walls cracked and fractured, and their roofs collapsed in heaps. Some structures had fallen completely, leaving only heaps of broken concrete and twisted metal. Road signs lay bent and unrecognizable, their letters warped and faded—faint traces of the world that had once been.

The destruction was everywhere he looked. Storefronts and homes were left in ruins, and overturned cars lined the streets, their shattered windows spilling glass across the road. An eerie silence filled the air, pressing down on him. It was as if time itself had stopped.

Jake reached into the suit's pocket and pulled out a

crumpled piece of paper, studying the hastily scribbled directions. Tom had given them to him over the radio, detailing how to find his home. Jake scanned the notes, tracing the path in his mind. He was looking for a ranch-style house on the outskirts of town. Tom had said the driveway would have a metal sign reading The Holdens, although he was unsure if it would still be intact after the impact.

After what seemed like hours, Jake finally reached the other side of town, his eyes landing on a driveway that matched Tom's description. The sign was still partially standing, though twisted in a bent mess. He walked down the cracked driveway, each step feeling heavier, a mix of trepidation and hope filling him as he neared the house.

As he reached the porch, he looked through a dust-covered window, peering into the darkness. Gathering himself, he pushed the door open, wincing as the rusted hinges let out a sharp squeal. He stepped inside, the loud rustling of his suit breaking the silence with each move he made.

Inside, the house was a wreck. Broken furniture lay scattered across the floor, and thick dust blanketed every surface. He moved carefully, stepping over debris and broken belongings, checking each room for signs of life. But the house remained silent and empty.

At last, he found a door leading down to the basement. He took a deep breath, steadied himself, and descended the creaky stairs, his boots echoing through the hollow silence. The basement was darker, a dense shadow covering every corner. He clicked on his flashlight, the beam cutting through the darkness as he scanned the area. Eventually, his light fell on a large steel door at the room's far end.

A faint voice crackled through a nearby speaker as he approached, sending a jolt through him. "Jake, is that you?"

Chapter 10

Emily's eyes were fixed on the door to the decontamination room, fighting against the tide of fear rising within her. Jake had disappeared through that door, leaving her alone in the sterile antechamber. Finally, she turned away, walking toward the elevator. Each step felt like she was moving farther from Jake, her tension growing. The elevator doors closed with a quiet thud, and as the cabin descended, her anxiety surged, forcing her to grip the handrail tightly to keep steady.

Thoughts whirled in her mind, each one adding to her growing unease. What if Jake didn't return? How would she lead the others? Jake knew the bunker's systems inside out, from the generators to the air filtration units. Over the last year, he'd taken time to show her and Frank the basics, but Emily worried their knowledge wouldn't be enough if Jake didn't return.

The elevator halted, and Emily entered the long tunnel to the waste management room. Shadows flickered in the dim light as she walked, her footsteps echoing in the stillness. She focused on each step, trying to avoid the darker thoughts that threatened to swallow her.

She neared the end of the tunnel and saw the heavy door ahead, standing like a sentinel over the bunker's secrets. She stepped through it with relief but jumped when a small voice spoke.

"Where's Jake?"

Emily turned, startled to see Lily standing in the shadows, her face anxious. "Lily," Emily managed, relief softening her tone. "What are you doing here?"

"I was looking for Jake," Lily said softly. "I saw both of you come down here, so I followed."

Emily knelt, her concern growing. "Lily, it's dangerous down here," she said gently. "There's a lot of equipment and machinery. It's not safe for you to be here alone."

Lily lowered her head, embarrassed. "I know, but… I wanted to ask Jake if he'd play a board game with me later." She fidgeted, looking at the closed door behind Emily. "I almost followed you down the tunnel, but it looked too dark and scary, so I waited here. Why didn't he come back with you?"

Emily hesitated, unsure how much she should reveal. Lily was wise, but Emily didn't want to tell her too much. The risks were too high, and she couldn't afford to let any concern ripple through the others.

"Jake's working on something important," Emily said finally, placing a comforting hand on Lily's shoulder. "He'll be back soon, but he's busy and can't be disturbed."

Lily nodded, but the worry in her eyes lingered. "Is the bunker safe?" she whispered.

Emily hesitated, feeling the weight of the question. "Yes, Lily," she replied with forced calm.

They stepped into the elevator, and as the doors slid shut, Emily felt a moment of calm. Lily's presence, even briefly, brought some reassurance. Despite her gnawing worries for Jake and the bunker's safety, she knew she couldn't let her fear take hold—her role as leader meant keeping solid and calm for everyone who relied on her.

* * *

Frank was briefing Daniel and Rob on the latest updates when he noticed Emily and Lily approaching.

His brows lifted in surprise. "Lily! I wondered where you were."

Lily looked up at Emily, searching for reassurance. Emily picked up on this and gave her a warm smile, stepping in to respond.

"She was with me," Emily said, lightly patting Lily's shoulder.

Frank nodded, relieved. "Good to know. I'll finish here with these guys, then catch up with you."

As he returned to his briefing, Lily glanced up at Emily, her expression grateful yet uncertain. "Thanks for not telling him," she whispered.

Emily squeezed her shoulder gently. "Stay up here, okay? No more sneaking around."

Lily nodded. "Okay, I promise."

As Lily walked away, Frank returned to Emily, his expression turning serious. "So, Jake's out there now?"

Emily sighed, looking away momentarily. "Yes, he left about twenty minutes ago. I can't help worrying. I hope he'll be alright."

Frank nodded thoughtfully, offering her a reassuring

smile. "He's trained for this. If anyone can handle it, it's him."

"I know," she replied, her voice softer. "But I keep thinking about the risks. Letting him go might put everyone in danger."

Frank shook his head. "You're too hard on yourself, Emily. Jake's spent time making sure we know enough to manage. Let's not think that way. He'll be back soon, safe and sound."

Emily felt a wave of relief. "You're right. I don't know why I'm so worried. He'll be back."

"There you go," Frank said, giving her shoulder a reassuring pat. "Remember, you're the reason we're all here and still surviving."

She managed a smile, grateful for his words. "Thank you, Frank. I'll check in on the others."

As the hours passed, Emily's thoughts kept drifting to Jake. She couldn't shake the feeling gnawing at her, a sense that deepened as time passed. It was a familiar feeling she'd known before on the day the asteroids struck. She remembered that gut-wrenching emptiness, the helplessness of realizing the world had changed irrevocably, that everything familiar had vanished. Now, that ache returned—a feeling that she had lost someone irreplaceable.

Chapter 11

As he stood in the basement of Tom's house, Jake fixed his gaze on the heavy steel door marking the entrance to Tom's shelter. Curiosity stirred inside him as he wondered what lay on the other side. He looked up at the camera mounted above the door, cleared his throat, and spoke into the silence of the basement. "I have suits for you," his voice echoed through the space, amplifying the stillness around him. "How do I get inside without exposing you to radiation?"

Tom's voice crackled through a speaker, filling the room with an unsettling sense of detachment. "As I said over the radio, I'm well-prepared down here," he replied, a trace of hesitation in his voice. "Except for the food situation..." he trailed off, leaving a heavy silence in his wake.

Jake nodded as he saw the door with its thick, fortified structure and complex locking mechanism. "Judging by the size of this door, it seems you spared no expense," he remarked.

Tom's calm, measured voice filled the basement again, breaking the silence. "Alright, Jake, let me walk you through the process," he began. "I'll open the door remotely so you can come inside. Once you're in, close the door and wait for me to lock it. Then, head down the hallway."

Tom's voice became slightly more animated as he explained the next steps. "You'll see a door on your right down the hall. That's the shower room. You'll need to rinse off your suit there to avoid bringing in any residual radiation."

He continued, "After you finish, I'll unlock the next door. From there, you'll enter a room where you can remove the suit. Then, follow the hallway to a door on the left. That's where I'll meet you."

As Jake listened, he couldn't help but feel a sense of awe at the sophisticated setup. He expected a basic shelter hidden beneath Tom's house, but this was far more elaborate than he had imagined.

Yet, as impressed as he was, a nagging feeling of unease tugged at the back of Jake's mind. There was something odd about the situation. How could someone who had built such a well-equipped shelter run out of food in just a year? He tried to shake off the feeling and focus on the task, but the unease persisted.

"You ready, Jake?" Tom's voice crackled over the speaker, pulling him back to the present.

"Yeah," Jake replied, "ready when you are."

After a brief pause, a loud buzz sounded, followed by the click of the lock disengaging. Jake gripped the door handle, pulling it open as his heart pounded.

Ahead of him lay a dimly lit hallway. He took a tentative step forward, then another, until he was fully inside. As he closed the door behind him, he heard the heavy lock click back into place.

Jake looked down the hallway as his eyes adjusted to the low light, spotting the door to the showers up ahead. He started forward, each step heavy with his questions for Tom.

As Jake reached the door to the showers, Tom's voice came over the speaker again. "Alright, Jake. Remember to scrub down thoroughly. I can't unlock the next door until the radiation detector gives the all-clear."

Radiation detectors in the showers? Jake thought, his apprehension growing. This shelter was even more advanced than he'd assumed.

He stepped inside the shower room and positioned himself under the showerheads. A loud buzz filled the room as the showers sprang to life, spraying water from all directions. Jake grabbed a nearby scrubber and carefully cleaned the suit. After he finished, the buzzer sounded again, and the water shut off, leaving only the faint sound of it draining away. Another loud click signaled the unlocking of the door.

"All clear," Tom said over the speaker.

Jake entered the next room, a well-lit space with a bench and lockers. He removed his suit, reassured by Tom's elaborate setup that any contamination had been effectively eliminated. He hung the suit in a locker and took a steadying breath.

Tom's voice came through the speaker once more, calm as before. "You alright in there, Jake?"

"Yeah, I'm good," Jake replied as he started down the next hallway.

"Almost there," Tom said. "It's the next door on your left."

As Jake approached, the door swung open, and he found himself face-to-face with a man who appeared to be in his mid-forties. "Hello there, Jake," the man said, smiling as he extended a hand. "I'm Tom."

Jake took Tom's hand and shook it firmly. "Your setup here…it's impressive," he said, still taking in the room around him.

Tom chuckled. "I believe in being prepared. Plus, I have a background in engineering, so building this shelter was second nature."

"An engineer, huh?" Jake said. "I've got some experience in it, too."

Tom grinned. "Small world."

Jake returned the smile, his eyes scanning the place. The room felt unexpectedly homey, with comfortable chairs and a large television mounted on the wall. Shelves lined with books and movies gave the space a lived-in feel, despite being underground.

Tom gestured toward a chair. "Please, make yourself comfortable. Can I get you something to drink? I've got water and some canned juice."

"Water's fine, thanks," Jake replied, settling into one of the chairs.

Tom disappeared into a small kitchenette, returning shortly with a glass of water.

"Say, Tom," Jake began, "where's your family?"

Tom's smile faded. "I'm sorry, Jake, I should've told you sooner. It's just me here."

Chapter 12

Three Days Before Impact

T om's car screeched into the driveway, leaving tire marks on the pavement as he pulled to a stop. He wasted no time, jumping out of the vehicle and sprinting to the front door. His heart was racing, thudding against his chest as he burst into the house.

"May! Nick!" he screamed, his voice echoing off the walls. "We have to leave now!"

May's heart skipped a beat at the urgency in Tom's voice. She had never heard him like this before. Fear crept up her spine as she raced into the living room to meet him.

"What's going on?" she cried out, her voice cracking with anxiety.

Tom grabbed her arm tightly, his grip almost painful as he pulled her towards the door. "I'll explain everything later," he panted, "but for now, we need to leave immediately. Where's Nick?"

May pulled away from Tom, trying to make sense of the situation. Tom was always gentle and kind-hearted, but now he was entirely different. The fear that had been building inside of her was now becoming unbearable.

"Tom, please tell me what's going on," she begged, her eyes pleading with him for an answer.

Tom took a deep breath and looked into May's eyes, trying to keep his fear at bay. "I need you to trust me," he said firmly. "I will explain everything later, but there is no time right now. Now tell me, where is Nick?"

"He's at the mall with his friends," May replied.

"Let's go," Tom said, reaching for her hand.

May pulled away again. "No, Tom, you are scari…"

"They're after me, May!" Tom screamed. "If you don't hurry up, we're all going to die. Now let's go!"

May stood frozen as her mind raced, trying to comprehend Tom's words.

"Please, May," Tom pleaded, reaching for her hand.

"Okay," she whispered, her voice shaking. "I'm coming."

Tom led her out of the house to the driveway, where his car was still idling. He opened the passenger door and motioned for her to get in.

"We need to move quickly before they catch up with us," he said. He got into the car and backed out of the driveway. The tires screeched as they took off down the road.

May sat in silence, her heart pounding as she tried to make sense of the situation. Who was after Tom? Why were they in danger? And most importantly, where were they going?

As they drove out of the neighborhood and onto the main road, Tom's eyes darted back and forth, looking for any signs of danger. "We need to get Nick and leave town," he said.

"Tom, please," May replied, touching his arm. "What's happening?"

Tom looked over at her and took a deep breath. "I didn't want to involve you or Nick in this," he said quietly, "but they found me. I don't know how, but they found me."

"Who found you?" May asked.

Tom looked at her and then back at the road as he

remained silent.

"Tom, please tell me what is going on," she urged. "Who are these people? What do they want with you?"

Tom took a deep breath. "I used to work for the government, doing some....things," he said cryptically. "Things I'm not proud of. I thought I left all of that behind me, but they don't forget. They found me, and they want me back."

May's mind raced as she tried to piece together the puzzle. Tom had always been tight-lipped about his past, but she had never imagined anything like this.

"Why would they want you back?" she asked.

"I don't know," Tom admitted, "but it's not good. I feel they won't let me walk away this time." He paused before saying. "At least not alive, and that's why we are all in danger."

May's heart plummeted as she struggled to comprehend the gravity of their situation. Fear pulsed through her veins. "What are we going to do?"

Tom's eyes darted nervously before pulling into the mall parking lot. "I know a place we can go," he said. "A remote town in the middle of nowhere. Nobody can find us there."

"How do you know they won't find us?" she asked.

Tom sighed heavily. "May, I know you don't

understand anything happening right now, and I can't express how sorry I am for that. But I need you to trust me and let me think. Let's just get Nick and get back on the road."

May felt helpless as she hung her head. "I'm sorry, Tom," she whispered. "I'll be quiet."

As they pulled into a parking space, Tom took her hand. "I love you, May," he said. "Just know that."

May's heart ached at his words. "I love you too," she replied. But did she? She didn't know anymore. This was not the man she loved.

"What does Nick do at the mall?" he asked.

"He's probably at the arcade with his friends," May said.

"I want you to stay here in the car," he told her. "I will run in and get him."

"Okay," May said, "please hurry."

Tom exited the car and quickly scanned the parking lot. The mall was packed with people bustling in and out, and Tom's anxiety grew as he made his way towards the arcade, searching for any signs of his son. He recognized Nick's friend Mike at a ticket counter machine.

"Hey Mike," he called out.

Mike looked up. "Hey Tom, how's it going?"

"Where's Nick?" Tom asked without hesitation.

Mike looked confused. "I thought he was with you," he said.

"What do you mean with me?" Tom asked, his heart pounding.

"Some guy came in here," Mike said. "He told Nick that there was an emergency with his dad and to go with him."

Tom's eyes widened in fear. "Did he say where they were going?" he asked desperately.

"No," Mike said, looking worried. "Is everything okay?"

"No, it's not," Tom said as he turned and ran out of the arcade. They were closing in on him. They were running out of time.

Tom rushed back to the car where May was waiting for him. As he opened the door and got in, he saw the tears streaming down May's face.

"Where's Nick?" she asked.

"They got him," Tom said, his voice heavy with sadness. "I was too late, May. I didn't see it coming."

May's hands flew to her face as she began to sob, her body shaking with grief. "Oh, my God," she said. "What are we going to do, Tom? How could they do this to us?"

"We have to get somewhere safe," Tom said, trying to keep his voice steady. "There's no way of knowing where he is right now, so the best thing to do is just get out of here and wait for them to contact me."

"We can't leave him behind!" May screamed. "He's our son, Tom. We have to do something!"

"I know, May," Tom said. "But if we look for him now, we'll only be in danger. We have to wait for them to make contact, and then we'll figure out what to do next."

May wiped her tears away and fixed Tom with a determined stare. "At least tell me where we're going," she said. "No more secrets, Tom. I want to know what's going on."

Tom started the car and backed out of the parking space. He threw the gear in drive and floored the pedal, the car lurching forward with a roar. As they screeched out of the parking lot, he turned to May. "I have another house," he said.

May looked at him in disbelief. "What? Another house?"

"Eight hours from here," Tom continued. "Under the house, I have a bunker."

May's eyes widened in surprise. "A bunker?" she

repeated with disbelief. "Why do we need a bunker, Tom? What's going on?"

Tom's hands tightened on the steering wheel as he tried to keep his voice steady. "Because I knew this day might come," he said. "I wanted us to be prepared. We'll be safe there until we figure out our next move."

"What is coming, Tom?" May pressed on.

"For all I know," Tom said, "the end of the world."

* * *

The car ride was tense over the next hour, with an eerie silence that filled the vehicle. Tom's eyes were fixed on the road ahead. He occasionally checked the mirrors, his instincts telling him to be extra cautious. They were on winding country roads, far from major highways or bustling city streets. Tom took every opportunity to switch directions, making sudden turns to shake off any possible followers that might be tailing them.

May sat motionless in the passenger seat, her gaze fixed out the window. The passing scenery was a blur as she was lost in her thoughts. Her mind was racing with worry and fear for their son's safety. Now and then, she wiped away a tear that rolled down her cheek. The silence between her and Tom was heavy, each lost in their own thoughts. She couldn't bear the uncertainty any longer and broke the silence.

"Tom," May said, her voice shaking. "Do you think they hurt him?"

He took a deep breath before answering, "I don't know, May. But we can't think about that right now. We must focus on getting to safety and finding out what they want from me."

May nodded in agreement, though the knot in her stomach remained. She leaned back in her seat, staring again blankly out the window. The minutes dragged on as they continued their journey.

As Tom made another turn onto a gravel road, he saw a flash of light in the mirror, and his stomach dropped.

"May," he said.

"What?" she replied.

"I think we're being followed," Tom said.

May looked at her side mirror, her eyes wide. "What? How do you know?"

"I saw a glimmer of light in the rearview mirror," Tom said. "I need you to hold on in case I need to make any sudden turns."

May's eyes darted between Tom and the mirror. "Do

you think it's them?" she asked.

"I don't know," Tom said. "But we're not going to take any chances."

"Tom, Nick could be with them," she said.

"No," he said firmly. "They would not bring him if they were following us. They would have him somewhere far away from us."

May's heart sank as she realized the truth of what Tom had said. If Nick wasn't with their pursuers, then where was he? Was he hurt? Scared? She wiped away another tear as they continued down the road.

"We need to get off this gravel road," Tom said. "The dust is giving away our location."

As Tom scanned the surroundings ahead, May pointed out the window. "There," she said, "Route 24 up ahead."

Tom saw the sign and made a quick decision. "Hang on," he said.

May gripped the dashboard as Tom made a sharp turn onto the road. As soon as the tires hit the pavement, he floored the pedal, his eyes fixed on the road ahead. But when he glanced in the rearview mirror again, his heart sank. The car behind them was much closer than before.

"It is them," May said, her voice trembling. "They

are catching up."

Tom's heart was racing as he saw the approaching car get closer in the rearview mirror.

"Open the glovebox," Tom told May, his voice shaking with adrenaline.

May's eyes widened as she looked at the glovebox. She hesitated for a moment before reaching over and opening it. Her hand jerked back when she saw what was in there.

"A gun, Tom?" May exclaimed in shock. "Why do you have a gun in here?"

"Just give it to me, May," Tom said sternly.

May's hand shook as she reached into the glovebox and picked up the gun. She handed it to Tom, her eyes glued to the mirror as the car behind them grew closer.

"Be careful," May said, her voice filling with concern.

"I can handle it," Tom replied.

In the heat of the moment, May had forgotten what Tom had said about his past. "Of course," she said.

Suddenly, the car behind them swerved and slowly crept up beside them. Tom kept his left hand tightly gripped on the steering wheel as he raised the gun with his right hand. May quickly ducked her head and held her ears as Tom fired the weapon.

May screamed as the shots rang out inside the car. "Tom!"

"Stay down!" he yelled back.

The pursuing car backed off momentarily before another shot rang out, this time from the driver chasing them. May screamed again as the bullet shattered their windshield, glass flying everywhere. As the car approached them again, Tom raised his gun once more; his eyes locked onto his target. He aimed and pulled the trigger. Immediately after the gun fired, the car beside them swerved and hit their car, sending it spinning out of control. Tom frantically turned the wheel to correct the car's orientation, but it was too late. The vehicle slid off the road and began tumbling over and over. Tom's head hit the window, and everything turned to chaos—sky, dirt, metal. For a moment, he couldn't think, couldn't breathe. His mind blanked as the world spun out of control.

* * *

Tom's eyes fluttered as he slowly came to. The sight before him was disorienting—the car had come to a stop, its front end crumpled, and steam billowed out from under the hood. He winced in pain as he called out for May. But there was no response. His panic grew as he realized that May wasn't in the car with him. Frantically unbuckling his seatbelt, he attempted to open the door, but it wouldn't budge. The crash had left it mangled and impossible to open. He scanned his surroundings, feeling trapped and helpless.

Flames suddenly erupted from the engine. The heat hit him full force as he scrambled to free himself. With no other option, he climbed out of the window, barely managing to pull himself out before falling to the ground with a painful cry.

The flames of the burning car continued to grow as he struggled to pull himself up from the ground. He stumbled away, his body wracked with pain, but he knew he needed to get as far away from the car as possible. He called out for May again, his voice hoarse and desperate, but there was still no response. He scanned the area for any sign of her, his heart pounding. The car was now fully engulfed in flames, casting a bright orange glow across the surrounding area.

Suddenly, he heard a faint cry in the distance and turned his head towards the sound. There, lying on the ground, was May. Relief washed over Tom as he began limping towards her. Finally, he reached her and collapsed to the ground beside her. The sight that greeted him was almost too much to bear. He pulled her onto his lap, his heart sinking as he saw the twisted metal protruding from her abdomen, blood seeping out of her wound.

"No, May," he cried out. "No, not like this."

He held her close, feeling her shallow breaths against his chest.

"Please find Nick," she managed to gasp.

"I will, May," he promised, tears flowing freely now. "I'll find him."

"Find him," May repeated, her voice fading. Her eyes closed, and he knew she was gone.

He held her close, rocking back and forth, his sobs filling the air. It was all his fault. His past caught up to him, and now his wife, who had nothing to do with it, was dead, and their son was missing.

Tom's heart was heavy with grief as he laid May's lifeless body down on the ground. He couldn't believe she was gone, and he knew deep down that he would never recover from the pain of losing her. But he had to be strong for Nick, who was still out there.

As he stood up, his eyes fell on the car that had been chasing them. He was surprised to see that it hadn't crashed but had stopped on the side of the road. He took a deep breath and began to limp towards the car. As he walked, he stepped on something hard. He looked down and saw his gun. It had flown out of his hand during the crash. He picked it up and slowly continued to the car.

He held the gun up as he crept his way around the back of the car to the driver's side. The man who had been chasing them was slumped over the steering wheel. As he got closer, he saw that his last shot had hit its target. He slowly opened the door and pulled the man out, and he fell lifelessly to the ground.

He looked back at the field where he left May and felt regretful. He couldn't leave her here like this. A bitter taste filled his mouth as he stepped away from the car. Each step back toward her felt heavier than the last, the weight of what had happened settling into his bones. The field was quiet now—too quiet—and she looked so small lying there, as if the world had already begun to forget her.

He crouched beside her and brushed the hair from her face. Her skin was cold, pale, and streaked with dirt. He hesitated, just for a second, then slid his arms beneath her and lifted her gently. Her body was limp, heavier than he remembered, and the tears came again —quiet, hot, and unwanted. He carried her to the car, opened the trunk, and laid her inside with as much care as he could manage. Then he closed it, stood there a moment longer, and finally got behind the wheel. As the engine rumbled to life, he took one last glance at the field behind him before turning onto the road toward the bunker—and whatever waited for him next.

Chapter 13

Present Day

Jake seethed with anger, his fists clenched and his shoulders tense. He'd risked everything to get to Tom's bunker, only to discover he had deceived him. He glared at Tom, anger brimming over as he fought to keep his voice steady. "What do you mean it's only you here?" he demanded. "You lied to get me here?"

Tom's face twisted with guilt. "Not entirely," he muttered.

"Not entirely?" Jake's voice rose. "I risked my life out there for you, Tom—risked everything for a family you don't even have!"

"No, wait!" Tom's hands shot up defensively. "Please, Jake. Just let me explain."

Jake exhaled sharply, forcing himself to step back, but his anger lingered. "This better be good," he growled. "You got me out here on a lie."

Tom's voice dropped, tinged with sorrow. "I did have a family," he said, the words catching in his throat. "My wife...she died. My son is missing. I don't even know if he's still alive. I've been down here alone since the impact."

Jake's anger eased slightly as he took in the weight of Tom's words, but he wasn't ready to trust him. "How did she die?" he asked. "And your son, why is he missing?"

Tom's face fell. "She got really sick down here, and we didn't have the medication that she needed. As for Nick..." his voice trailed off. "Look around, Jake. What good would talking about it do?"

Despite his initial fury, Jake couldn't shake a creeping sympathy. He took in the scene around him— the meticulously organized supplies and carefully maintained equipment. "How could you be running low on food if you've been down here alone?"

"I didn't lie about that," Tom replied. "If my family

were still here, we would have run out months ago."

Jake's eyes narrowed. "Then how were you not prepared?" he pressed. "With a setup like this, how do you miss the most important part of survival?"

Tom sighed, "I never thought I'd be down here like this for so long. I tried to prepare, but it just…wasn't enough."

"Why should I trust anything you're telling me?" Jake asked. "You already lied to get me here, Tom. How do I know you're not lying again?"

Tom looked defeated. "Because I had no choice," he said. "If I had told you the truth, you wouldn't have come."

"Maybe I would've come," Jake shot back in defense. "Ever think of that?"

Tom shook his head, meeting Jake's eyes. "No," he replied. "I don't think you would have."

Jake's mind raced, processing everything he had been told. "You mentioned reaching out to others," he said. "What did you mean by that?"

"I tried contacting other survivors," Tom explained. "There are people out there, Jake—people in shelters, in community bunkers. But they all turned me down."

"Why?" Jake asked.

Tom's voice took on a bitter edge. "Because I'm just

one man out here alone in a dead world," he said. "Not worth the risk, I suppose."

Jake's understanding deepened slightly. "I saw suits in the lockers," he said, suddenly realizing that he had brought extra suits for nothing. "Did you go outside?"

"There's no use," Tom said bitterly. "Imagine me wandering up to another shelter in a radiation suit. They would never open the doors for me."

Jake checked his watch, remembering his obligation to Emily. "Where's your radio?" he asked abruptly.

"Follow me," Tom said, leading him to a room filled with radio equipment. Computers hummed, layers of dust gathering along the consoles, and wires tangled across the surface of the tables.

"How far can this reach?" Jake asked.

Tom's eyes scanned the equipment. "Not sure," he admitted. "I never really tested it's full potential."

Jake's eyes moved to a staircase tucked in the corner of the room. "What's down there?" he asked.

Tom hesitated. "Storage, supplies, food…my wife."

"I'm sorry," Jake's voice softened.

"Thanks," Tom replied.

Jake sat down at the radio. "I need to check in," he said. "If you don't mind, would you step out of the room for a moment?"

"Sure," Tom said. "Take all the time you need."

* * *

Emily sat by the radio, fingers tapping rhythmically on the edge of the desk. Jake was already fifteen minutes overdue to check in, and the anxiety gnawing at her grew sharper by the minute. She'd tried to distract herself by keeping busy with supply counts and inventory throughout the day, but now there was nothing left to do but wait.

Footsteps echoed down the hall, and she looked up to see Frank standing in the doorway, his expression of mirrored concern.

"Anything yet?" he asked.

Emily shook her head. "No, not yet." She replied. "I'm getting worried, Frank."

He moved closer, resting a reassuring hand on her shoulder. "Jake will call. He's strong and one of the best we've got. If anyone can make it out there and back, it would be him."

A smile crossed her lips. "I hope so," she murmured. "But what if something happened? What if he's hurt?"

Frank squeezed her shoulder gently. "We can't think

that way, Em. Trust me. He will be back soon."

She nodded, trying to control her worry, and then noticed something unusual in Frank's expression. "Frank," she started, "is there something else on your mind?"

He looked away for a moment, then back at her. "Emily, there's something I need to tell you," he said.

"What is it?" Emily asked.

Frank took a breath. "Jane and I…we're expecting."

Emily's eyes widened in surprise. "Frank, that's amazing!" She embraced him with a hug.

But even as the joy settled in, she realized the gravity of what this meant. The thought of bringing a new life into this harsh reality was terrifying.

"Congratulations," she said softly. "Don't worry yourself, Frank. Sarah's here, and she's a good doctor. She'll make sure Jane and the baby get through this."

"I know," Frank nodded, "but it's hard to imagine raising a baby here."

Emily placed a comforting hand on his arm. "Lily will be thrilled. And you're not alone, Frank. We're all here with you."

Suddenly, the radio crackled to life. "Emily, are you there?"

Emily's heart leaped, and she quickly grabbed the

mic. "Jake! I'm here. Are you alright?"

"Yeah, I'm fine," he said. "I'm at Tom's shelter."

Emily exhaled, a surge of relief flooding her system. "When are you coming back?"

"I'll rest a bit here," Jake replied, "then we'll suit up and head back."

"Be careful, Jake," she said. "We'll all be waiting for you."

"Don't worry," he replied, "I'll be back soon."

The radio fell silent again. Emily put the mic back down on the desk and looked up at Frank. "At least we know now that he's ok."

Frank smiled. "See? What did I tell you?"

"Yeah, yeah," Emily replied. "Don't worry this, don't worry that."

"I'm just saying." Frank said, holding his hands up, "You stress yourself out more than you need to be."

Emily nodded in agreement. "Yeah, I need to work on that."

* * *

Jake carefully set the mic down and got up from the desk. He walked into the other room, where Tom was patiently waiting for him. "If I'm bringing you back with me," Jake began, "I need more answers. Tell me, how did you build all this?"

Tom's expression shifted to confusion. "What do you mean?" he asked.

Jake crossed his arms. "Explain your work. I need to know how and why you have all of this."

Tom hesitated but finally began to speak. "I had a company," he said. "We specialized in underground shelters for both private clients and the government. The bunker you and your people are in? I helped build it—until the government suddenly pulled out and terminated the contract."

Jake's pulse quickened. "How do you know which bunker we're in?"

Tom looked at the TV mounted on the wall. "It was all over the news," he said. "Before the impact, the media showed footage of the bunker. I saw the soldiers, and when you showed up here today, I recognized you."

Jake's eyes narrowed. "Why should I believe you?"

Tom held his gaze. "Because I have nothing left to lose. I swear, Jake, I'm telling you the truth."

"Alright," Jake said. "But understand, you've lied more than once already."

"I know," Tom replied. "And I'm sorry. But I had no other choice."

"Suit up," Jake instructed. "We leave in twenty minutes."

Jake wondered if he was making the right call. But in today's world, choices were often between bad and worse.

* * *

Emily stood with Frank beside her, nerves stretched thin. "They all need to know," she said.

"You're ready for this?" he asked.

She nodded, taking a deep breath. "Jake will be back soon with Tom and his family. People will see them and panic if we're not upfront."

Frank's gaze softened. "I'll be right beside you. They trust you, Em."

She pressed the intercom button. "Everyone, please gather in the meeting area. I have an important announcement to make."

People assembled, faces filled with curiosity. Emily looked over them, feeling the weight of responsibility bearing down.

"Jake left the bunker to help survivors," she began.

The crowd murmured, questions bubbling to the surface.

"Jake went outside?" someone asked.

"Did you open the doors?" another questioned.

"Please," Frank interjected, raising his hands. "Let Emily explain."

Emily took another deep breath. "Jake made radio contact with survivors. He has everything he needs to protect himself out there. This bunker has a decontamination room for when he returns. We will continue to be safe and isolated from the conditions outside the bunker."

The tension in the room seemed to ease up. A woman stepped forward. "Thank you for letting us know," she said. "Any ideas when they will be back?"

Emily smiled. "Very soon."

Chapter 14

"We're here," Jake announced as they approached the hatch to the bunker.

"I know," Tom replied.

"Right," Jake said. "You've been here before."

He reached down, flipped the panel open, and punched in the key code to unlock the hatch. As he pulled the hatch open, scraping metal echoed, breaking the quiet. "After you," he said, gesturing for Tom to descend first.

Tom hesitated, glancing down into the open hatch, then looking back at Jake with a sober expression. "Listen, Jake," he said, "thank you for helping me. You didn't have to, but you did."

"Just don't make me regret it," Jake replied. "Now go. We need to get out of this."

Tom nodded. He took a breath and descended the ladder, his movements steady but tense. Jake followed close behind, casting one last look at the barren landscape around them before pulling the hatch shut and locking it.

Once they reached the floor, they moved quietly into the decontamination room. Jake opened the door, motioning for Tom to follow him in, and as soon as they both stepped inside, he closed it, sealing the heavy metal door behind them. Turning to the control panel, he pressed a button, and instantly, powerful water jets sprang from all directions, enveloping them in a dense, vigorous spray.

The cold and forceful water washed over them, scrubbing away the invisible dust and radiation that clung to their suits. Jake stood still under the jets, the water numbing but strangely calming as it cascaded down. His thoughts, however, were far from calm as he mentally ran through everything that had happened and the implications of bringing Tom into their sanctuary.

Once thoroughly cleaned, the water shut off abruptly, leaving only the sound of dripping water as they stepped out. They took their suits off and entered the elevator. As they stood in the confined space, the lift hummed to life.

"So, how's the bunker holding up?" Tom asked, breaking the silence.

Jake glanced over at him, "I've had to install a few things here and there, but so far, it's holding up."

Tom gave a short nod. "I never did see it again after they stopped the build," he replied. "Lucky you that they left everything inside. You would've been left with nothing if they'd cleaned it before abandoning it."

"Yeah," Jake replied. "Lucky us."

The elevator continued its slow descent, the silence between them punctuated only by the low whirring of the machinery. They finally reached the waste management level, and the doors opened. They stepped into the long, dimly lit tunnel. The familiar scent of metal and concrete hit Jake, reminding him of how cut off they were from the outside world.

"This place is pretty big," Tom commented, his voice echoing slightly as they walked. "Shame I couldn't finish it. I would've loved this place instead of the shelter I had."

"Let's just get up there and see Emily," Jake said.

The name seemed to catch Tom off guard, and he

turned to Jake with a raised brow. "Emily?" he repeated.

"She's the leader here," Jake said. "She'll decide what to do with you."

Tom frowned. "What to do with me?" he echoed. "Should I be worried?"

Jake's gaze held steady. "We'll see," he replied. "She's expecting your wife and son. What she'll get is a liar."

"I get the feeling that you haven't forgiven me," Tom said.

"Not entirely," Jake replied. "Keep moving."

They exited the tunnel to the waste management area and stepped into the next elevator. Once on the main level, Jake led Tom to Emily's office, where she sat at her desk, deep in concentration. The instant she looked up, her face broke into a relieved smile.

"Jake, you're back!" she exclaimed, standing and moving towards him. She wrapped her arms around him in a welcoming embrace.

Jake returned the hug, feeling the tension release slightly from his shoulders. When Emily finally pulled back, her gaze turned to Tom.

"And you must be Tom," she said, extending her hand.

Tom accepted her handshake. "Pleasure to meet

you,"

Emily glanced around as if she was searching for something, or rather, someone.

Tom caught her unspoken question and took a deep breath. "I know what you're thinking," he said quietly. "Let me explain the family situation."

He began to recount his story, his tone subdued as he detailed his time in isolation, his wife's tragic passing, and the uncertainty around his son's fate. Jake remained a silent observer, watching Tom's face closely, alert to any signs of deceit.

After a moment, Emily spoke, her expression softening. "Well, now," she said, "I can't imagine what it would be like to face that kind of isolation alone."

"Thank you for understanding," Tom replied.

"No problem," she said. "Let me talk to Jake briefly, and we'll get you settled."

She motioned for Jake to join her outside the office, her expression intense. Once they were alone in the hallway, she turned to him. "I don't trust him," she admitted.

"Neither do I," Jake agreed.

"What made you decide to bring him here?" she asked.

Jake leaned against the wall, folding his arms. "I

think there's more going on in his bunker than he's letting on."

"You want to go back out there?" Emily asked with a hint of worry.

"I need to find out," he replied. "I saw a set of stairs. He claimed it was a storage room, but something about his answer didn't sit right."

"So, what do we do with him?" Emily asked.

Jake replied, "We'll have to keep him locked in a room until we know for sure."

They returned to the office, where Tom looked up with a hopeful smile. "Everything good?" he asked.

"All good," Emily replied. "Let's get you to a room so you can get comfortable."

Emily led Tom down the corridor toward a vacant room, with Jake close behind.

"Here you go," Emily said, gesturing to the door. Tom paused, glancing at the room, then back at her. "Am I not staying on the residential level?"

"They're all full right now," Jake replied. "We're already overcrowded."

"Ah, I see," Tom said. "That would explain it."

"It's just until we can figure something else out," Emily said.

Tom stepped into the room. He paused for a

moment, turning around to face Emily. "Thanks for bringing me here," he said. "It really means alot."

Emily nodded. "No problem," she replied. "Get some rest now. It's been a long day."

As Tom took a seat on a nearby chair, Emily closed the door. A few second's later, he heard the faint click of the lock.

* * *

Jake and Emily stood by the entrance of the decontamination room. Emily's worry was evident in her eyes. "Are you sure you want to go back out there?" she asked.

"I was fine the first time," he replied. "I'll be fine again."

Emily's voice trembled. "Tom's already agitated. I hope the lock holds."

"I spoke with Frank," Jake said. "He'll set up shifts with Rob and Daniel to keep an eye on him."

"Thanks, Jake," Emily said. "People are starting to ask questions."

"They'll understand," Jake replied. "We're doing this for everyone's safety."

Emily nodded. "I hope this turns out okay. And I

hope you find nothing more than storage."

"Me too," Jake murmured. "But I need to be sure." As Jake started to open the decontamination door, Emily's pulse quickened. "Jake, wait," she called.

He turned, surprised, as she caught up to him. She paused momentarily before wrapping her arms around him, pulling him close, and pressing her lips to his in a sudden kiss.

Jake was startled but quickly returned the embrace, his arms encircling her. Their kiss was brief but filled with an unspoken bond.

As Emily pulled back, Jake held her a moment longer, a gentle smile forming. "Well, now," he said. "What was that all about?"

She smiled back, her voice soft. "Last time, I didn't get to say goodbye."

Jake held his gaze to hers. "Goodbye, Emily," he said. "I'll be back soon."

With one final look, Jake turned away and stepped into the room. Emily did the best she could to hold back her tears as the door shut behind him.

* * *

Jake's approach to Tom's bunker was filled with

foreboding. Something wasn't right, and he intended to find out what it was. He stepped cautiously onto the porch, but a shift in the floor made him pull back, not wanting to risk any damage to his suit. He somehow managed to miss the extensive damage to the porch when he was here before. He felt lucky that he didn't fall through the first time.

He slowly crept around to the back door, and as he passed a nearby tree, his gaze landed on something that stopped him in his tracks. A cross stood against the tree, weathered and etched with a name—May. The realization dawned on Jake with grim clarity. Tom had lied again; his wife wasn't in the bunker.

"Damn it," Jake muttered.

He proceeded to the back door, testing its sturdiness before pushing it open. Inside, he moved with caution, navigating through the rooms until he reached the basement. Standing before the steel door, he punched in the key code he had memorized when Tom wasn't aware he was watching. The lock clicked, and the door creaked open.

He stepped inside, cleaning off in the decontamination room before moving to the main shelter area. His eyes locked onto the staircase in the radio room. He descended the stairs, curious about what he would find in the next room.

At the bottom, he encountered another steel door. Entering the code again, he opened it, revealing a pitch-black space. He found a switch and flicked it on. The sight before him was staggering.

Rows of monitors, charts, and diagrams lined the walls. Jake walked over to a stack of papers and started scanning over them. It wasn't long before he began piecing together the truth—Tom worked for the government.

On a desk lay a newspaper article detailing the events of the incoming asteroids. One photo caught his attention—a shot of their bunker gates, and he saw himself among the crowd. He continued to search shelves and drawers until something caught his eye on a nearby monitor.

"Operation Impact," he read out loud.

As he continued reading what was on the screen, his eyes widened. "This is it," he whispered to himself.

* * *

Tom paced his room at the bunker. "I need some water," he called out.

Rob didn't budge. "You'll have to wait until Daniel

gets here. I can't leave you alone."

Tom scoffed. "Come on, man, I'm dying of thirst here."

"Can't do it," Rob replied.

Just then, Emily walked into the room. "How's everything here?" she asked.

"All good," Rob replied. "Just water requests on repeat."

Emily shook her head. "Let him wait. We need to be cautious until Jake's back."

"Understood," Rob said.

Emily was about to leave the room when suddenly, Jake stormed in, his face hard, eyes blazing with anger. Emily barely managed a greeting as he pushed past her, his focus unbreakable. She followed him, knowing something was very wrong.

"Unlock the door," Jake demanded as he reached Tom's room. Rob complied, and Jake entered, zeroing in on Tom.

"Hey, Jake, what's—"

Tom's words were cut off as Jake grabbed him by the throat, slamming him against the wall.

"Who are you?" Jake shouted.

"Whoa, Jake, calm down," Tom replied, holding his arms up.

"WHO ARE YOU?" Jake demanded again.

"What's happening?" Emily cried as she rushed into the room.

Jake tightened his grip on Tom. "You lied! You work for the government! There were no asteroids!"

Emily gasped, covering her mouth. "What did you just say?"

Jake's voice became terrifyingly quiet. "There were never any asteroids," he said. "They were nuclear bombs."

Chapter 15

Two Days Before Impact

Tom guided the car into the driveway, his head throbbing from the events that took place earlier. He surveyed the property carefully, eyes scanning every corner for signs of danger. He had discarded his phone after the crash, ensuring there was no way they could track him here. Satisfied that he was alone, he stepped out of the car, wincing as pain flared up in his leg with each step. The house loomed before him, its darkened windows staring back emptily.

Taking a deep breath, Tom entered the house and limped to the bathroom. He opened the medicine cabinet with shaky hands, hoping to find relief from the pounding in his head. But the shelves were bare.

Frustrated, he cursed under his breath. Of course there was no medication. It had been months since he had last been here, months since he had restocked any supplies. But he had one more option—the bunker.

Steadying himself, he moved to the hidden entrance at the back of the house. With practiced fingers, he punched in the key code. A soft click confirmed the door had unlocked, and he pulled it open, revealing the dimly lit staircase that led to the underground shelter. A waft of musty air hit him as he stepped inside, shadows stretching along the walls as he made his way to the main quarters and flicked on a light.

He rummaged through the shelves, his fingers closing around a bottle of painkillers. Popping a few into his mouth, he swallowed dry, grateful for the quick relief. But as the physical discomfort eased, a more profound, sharper ache remained—a pain that pills couldn't touch. The memory of May, lifeless and cold in the car's trunk, stabbed through him. He had to bury her and give her the rest she deserved.

Slowly, Tom climbed back up the stairs and to the car. Opening the trunk, he hesitated momentarily, his heart clenching at the sight of her still form. Gently, he lifted her out and carried her to the backyard, laying her beside the old oak tree. He limped his way to the shed to retrieve a shovel, feeling the weight of loss press down on him with every step.

As he returned to the tree, tears began streaming down his face, blurring his vision. He remembered everything that had led to this moment. How did they find him? Why couldn't they have just left him in peace?

With each plunge of the shovel into the earth, he relived their shared memories. The backyard was quiet, and each shovelful of dirt seemed to echo louder in the silence. It felt as if he were not only burying May but also a part of himself. He dug deeper as though he could somehow bury the pain along with her.

Finally, he set the shovel aside and knelt by her body. Carefully, he picked her up and laid her into the grave. He whispered a short prayer, his voice catching on each word, before he began filling the grave. As he spread the last bit of soil over her, he sighed, exhausted and empty. May was at peace now, but his work was just beginning. He couldn't let her death be for nothing. Before he could act, he needed rest. It had been a long, brutal day, and pain still coursed through his body. Wiping his tears, he took a shaky breath, heading back inside. He returned to the bunker, secured the lock behind him, and collapsed onto the cot. Within minutes, exhaustion overtook him, pulling him into a deep, dreamless sleep.

* * *

Tom's eyes snapped open, his heart racing. For a split second, he hoped it had all been a nightmare—that he'd wake up to find May by his side and Nick's laughter echoing through the house. But as his eyes adjusted to the dim, windowless space, reality crashed over him. He was still alone, buried in the bunker.

Tom sat up, rubbing his face, his muscles stiff from the rough cot. He knew he couldn't waste any more time. Operation Impact was real, and he knew exactly what was at stake. They had come after him for a reason. But the previous day's events puzzled him, a question lingering like an itch he couldn't scratch. If they needed him, why did they try to kill him?

A surge of urgency pushed him to his feet. He descended a staircase to a lower room. He punched in the access code, and the door opened. He stepped inside and switched on the lights, flooding the room with an intense brightness. He took a moment to survey the space, remembering all the years he had spent preparing here. After leaving the organization, he built this bunker and equipped it with the latest technology. It was the only way to stay one step ahead of them. But did he miss something?

He moved from chart to chart, meticulously poring over years of collected data. He scanned each piece of information before turning to his computer screens, hoping to find the clue he had overlooked. The mystery gnawed at him. His eyes burned from hours of reading, and just as he was about to step away, a soft beep pulled him back to the screen.

The hack he was running on the organization was finally completed, and new documents were loaded onto the monitor. He rubbed his tired eyes and leaned forward, dread pooling in his stomach as he read. The bombs that he had designed for them years ago were ready, and in just two days, they were going to drop them worldwide.

Tom's blood ran cold. The scale of destruction would be catastrophic. It was too late to stop the bombs. He had to warn people and give them a chance to prepare. Even if it was only a faint hope, it was better than no hope.

He sprinted to the adjacent room, where the most

advanced AI technology he had gathered over the years awaited him.

Sitting down, he began typing furiously, his fingers a blur as he worked to hack into the satellite network. It was a challenge that had taken him years to master, but now, there was no room for error.

The minutes that passed felt like hours, but eventually, a message flashed on the screen:

ACCESS GRANTED

He set up his camera, positioned it carefully before him, and activated the feed. He typed in a warning message, then hit record. The warning flashed, and suddenly, an AI president appeared on the screen. He took a deep breath and began to speak.

"My fellow Americans and people of the world..."

Chapter 16

Present Day

Jake held Emily tightly in his arms as they lay in bed, her head resting on his chest as she listened to the steady rhythm of his heartbeat. The room was silent, except for the sound of their breathing. After a few moments, Jake gently brushed her hair out of her eyes and spoke softly, "I didn't mean to scare you earlier."

Emily let out a small sigh as she recalled the day's events. Her mind drifted back to when Jake burst into Tom's room. She had never seen him so angry before, but she knew why.

"It's okay," she finally said. "But do you believe it was nuclear bombs?

"I'm sure," he replied. "There's no doubt in my mind what I saw on that computer."

Emily shuddered. "I just can't believe that the government would do something like that," she said. "And to think our president was willing to lie to us about asteroids."

Jake sat up in bed, his eyes filled with uncertainty as he spoke. "Oddly enough," he said, "I'm not so sure I want to fully believe the government or the president had anything to do with it. I don't trust Tom for one second, but there has to be more to this."

Emily shifted closer to Jake "What are you thinking?"

"I don't know," Jake replied. "I need to talk to Tom some more, but I can't right now. I need a few days to think before I go back in that room with him. Maybe in the meantime, I'll check out his bunker again and find out everything I can related to this Operation Impact."

Emily nodded, understanding Jake's need to step back and gather his thoughts. She had already admitted her feelings for Jake, and the idea of him leaving again was almost unbearable. But she knew that they had to get to the bottom of this.

She snuggled up closer to him, finding comfort in his arms. She kissed his lips softly, hoping to alleviate some of the tension weighing heavily on them both.

"Let's just try to get some sleep," she whispered. "We can start fresh tomorrow. You've had a long day already, Jake. Don't stay up all night stressing about this."

Jake nodded in agreement, grateful for Emily's calming presence. "You're right," he murmured. "We're not going anywhere anytime soon."

* * *

Emily woke up the following day to find that Jake was not in bed beside her. She sat up, feeling a sense of unease wash over her. There was only one reason why Jake would get up without her. He must have gone to Tom's bunker again. She got out of bed and quickly dressed, then went to the kitchen, where Frank was already sitting at the table with his coffee.

"Good morning, Emily," he said. "What brings you up so early?"

Emily leaned against the counter and crossed her arms. "Jake's gone again. He went to Tom's bunker without telling me."

Frank raised an eyebrow. "Ah, I see. Well, it'll be alright. I'm sure he had his reasons."

"He does," Emily replied. "I wish he would have told me though. We're supposed to be a team, right?"

Frank nodded. "I understand how you feel. But given the information we just found out about Tom and the bombs, maybe Jake thought you would try to stop him from going."

"Who's watching Tom right now?" Emily asked.

"Daniel is," Frank said.

Emily nodded. "How is Jane doing?"

Frank smiled, "She's feeling better after seeing Sarah yesterday. She's not as worried about going through pregnancy in the bunker as much as she was before."

"That's great to hear," Emily said.

Frank chuckled. "Speaking of babies, Jane and I told Lily about it, and she's excited to have a little brother or sister."

Emily grinned. "That's wonderful news. I'm so happy for her."

Frank finished his coffee and checked his watch. "Well, I have to go do my rounds now."

"Alright," Emily said. "I'm going to go talk to Tom for a bit."

Frank shook his head, "Maybe you should wait until Jake gets back before you talk to him."

"No, it's okay," Emily said. "I'll be fine. Daniel will be there."

"Alright, then," Frank said, grabbing his bag. "Just be careful. See you later, Emily."

"Bye, Frank," she replied.

She took a deep breath and went to Tom's room. She could maybe get him to talk if Jake wasn't around to intimidate him. She saw Daniel standing outside the room, his expression cautious as he spotted her.

"Hey, Daniel," she said, trying to sound casual.

"Emily?" Daniel said, looking surprised. "What brings you here?"

"I need to talk to Tom," Emily said.

"Where's Jake at?" Daniel asked.

"He went back out again," Emily said.

Daniel frowned. "You really shouldn't go in there alone," he warned.

"I'll be okay," Emily said. "I need to talk to him alone."

Daniel hesitated for a moment before reluctantly nodding. "Fine," he said. "But I'll be right outside the door if you need me."

He unlocked the door and opened it. Emily stepped

inside, feeling a chill run down her spine as the door shut behind her. Tom was lying on a makeshift bed that she had provided for him. He slowly sat up and looked at Emily. "No Jake?"

Emily shook her head. "Just me. Can we talk?"

Tom sat up. "What do you want?"

"Can I sit down?" Emily asked, gesturing towards the chair by the bed.

Tom shrugged. "Help yourself."

Emily sat down. "Listen, Tom, I need you to tell me what's going on. What's with all the secrets?"

Tom looked away, his face twisted in anger. "What's the use?" he spat. "You won't believe it anyway."

"We'll see about that," Emily said. "Just tell me about the nuclear bombs. Were there really no asteroids?"

Tom shook his head. "No asteroids," he said. "I can promise you that."

"Then tell me what happened," Emily said. "Just talk, and I'll listen."

Tom let out a deep sigh. "Well, prepare yourself because this is one hell of a story," he said.

* * *

Jake's heart raced as he arrived near Tom's house, determined to uncover the truth about Operation Impact and the nuclear bombs that had decimated the world. As he approached, he noticed something odd. Cars were parked outside Tom's house—cars he didn't recognize.

Confused, he slowly crouched behind a nearby tree and watched, his eyes scanning the area for any signs of life. Then, people emerge from the house. But something was off. They were not wearing any radiation suits.

What is going on here? Jake thought. Why are they not wearing suits? He watched as the people walked several feet from the house and stood there.

"What are they doing?" he muttered to himself.

Suddenly, there was a loud explosion, and the house collapsed, sending a cloud of dust and debris into the air. Jake jumped back in shock before quickly crouching back down behind the tree.

As he watched the dust settle, the people returned to the house. They descended the stairs to the basement, disappearing from view. After a few minutes, they emerged from the basement, talked some more, got in their cars, and left, leaving behind a smoldering heap of rubble where Tom's house had once stood.

Jake sat there, reeling from what he had just witnessed. After a few minutes, he looked around and slowly made his way to the house, the crunching of gravel under his boots the only sound in the stillness.

He descended the stairs to the basement, his heart pounding with anticipation. The bunker door was opened and mangled. He peered inside, and his heart sank as he realized why those people had been there. They thought Tom was in the bunker when they blew it open.

A growing sense of urgency filled his thoughts as he returned from the basement. He had to get back to Tom and learn more about what was happening. He was done playing around. It was time to find out who Tom was and, most importantly, what Operation Impact was about.

* * *

Emily sat there, her eyes fixated on Tom as he revealed the horrifying truth about the nuclear bombs. Her heart sank as she struggled to understand the magnitude of what he was saying. This couldn't be happening.

"If what you're saying is true," Emily said, "that is the most heinous thing I have ever heard."

"It will only get worse," Tom said. "There's nothing that can be done about it either."

"We have to tell Jake when he returns," Emily said.

Tom chuckled bitterly. "Like he will ever believe it."

"I believe you," Emily said. "As difficult as it is to accept, I believe you. Just let me talk to him first. I'm sure he'll understand once he knows what's happening."

"I hope so," Tom said.

Emily stood up. As she reached for the door, Tom called out to her. "Emily," he said.

She turned around. "Yes?"

"I'm so sorry for everything," Tom said. "For lying to you. I just needed to get to a safe place."

"You did what you had to do," Emily said.

"I know," Tom replied.

With a final nod, Emily opened the door and stepped out of the room, closing it softly behind her.

* * *

Jake stepped into the decontamination room, turned on the water, and thought about the people at Tom's house. They were not wearing radiation suits. He shook his head, trying to make sense of it all. The readings were off the charts, and he couldn't imagine anyone risking exposure to that level of radiation.

He cleaned himself off, removed his suit, and went to the elevators. As he ascended, his thoughts shifted to Emily. He had left her that morning without telling her he was going back out, and he knew she would be upset. He made a mental note to talk to her before seeing Tom. As the elevator doors opened, he was relieved to find Emily waiting.

"So," she said, crossing her arms. "You're back now?"

Jake rubbed the back of his neck, "Yeah, I'm back," he said.

Emily stood there for a moment, staring at Jake before finally stepping forward and embracing him. Jake wrapped his arms around her and held her tightly, grateful for the comfort of her embrace.

When they finally parted, Jake smiled. "So, you're not upset?" he asked.

"Oh, I'm upset," Emily said, smiling back. "But I missed you more."

"I'm sorry I didn't tell you I was going out," Jake said. "I had to see Tom's bunker again."

"It's okay," Emily said. "Just don't make a habit of it."

"I won't," Jake said. "Tom's bunker is gone."

Emily's expression shifted to confusion, "What do you mean gone?"

"I saw people there," Jake said, looking around to ensure no one was eavesdropping. "They blew it up."

Emily's eyes widened with shock, "Are you serious? Who were they?"

"I don't know," Jake said, shaking his head. "But they weren't wearing suits."

"Well," Emily said, "there is an explanation for that."

"What do you mean?" Jake asked.

"I talked to Tom," Emily said.

Jake's heart skipped a beat. "You talked to him alone?"

"Don't worry," Emily said. "Daniel was there. Look, Tom told me some things, and I believe him. It would be best if you heard what he has to say. I think it will explain this whole mess of a world we're in right now."

"You really think so?" Jake asked.

"He's the only one who has answers right now," Emily said. "And you need to hear them. Trust me."

Jake looked into Emily's eyes and saw the depth of

her conviction.

"Okay," he said. "Let's go talk to him."

* * *

Tom looked at Jake across the room. "Are you ready for this?" he asked.

"Ready as I'll ever be," Jake replied.

Tom took a deep breath. "Okay, here goes," he said. "Like I told you before, I worked in designing bunkers and shelters. That part was true. I didn't tell you that I was designing military weapons in the army before that. I joined the army when I was twenty. Eventually, my skills as an engineer and developer came in handy for military defense. I was a weapon engineer for many years before I decided to leave the army. I didn't do much after that. I lived alone and kept to myself."

Tom continued. "Sixteen years ago, I got a knock on my door. I answered to a man named Compton. He told me that a highly classified project needed my assistance and that if I came out of retirement for just a few years and helped them, I would be set for life. Now, I was already set for life, but as I said, I didn't do much, so I thought, why not."

Jake stared at Tom. "This was Operation Impact,

right?" he asked.

Tom nodded his head. "Correct, Operation Impact. Now, I didn't know what it was at the time. I just thought I was returning to the military for a few more years for one last project. I had seen the news about the issues with China and Russia, so for all I knew, we were on the brink of another big war. If anything, I was doing my part to help protect our country."

Jake nodded. "So what happened after the house visit?" he asked.

"I was told to wait a few days, and I would be picked up," Tom said. "So a few days later, a car came, and off I went. They took me to the airport, and we flew out to some remote island. They put me to work right away. They wanted me to help them design a bomb, not just any bomb like the rest of them. This one was special. It would contain RDA. Short for Radiological Deception Agent."

Jake stared at the floor for a moment before looking up at Tom. "So what does this agent do?"

Tom hung his head. "It is a substance that creates high-level readings on radiation detectors but is completely harmless."

Jake stood up and began pacing the room. "So you

are telling me that the radiation on the surface is not actually radiation but some agent designed to mimic radiation?"

"Yes," Tom said. "That's exactly what it is. RDA was created by combining several harmless elements and compounds in a specific way that would mimic the signature of ionizing radiation. Scientists tested the substance extensively to ensure that it would consistently trigger radiation detectors without actually causing harm to human health."

Jake shook his head. "We've been living down here all this time, and it was safe up there?"

Emily noticed that Jake was getting upset. "Just keep listening to him," she said. "There is a lot more."

Tom continued. "Now, remember, I still didn't know what I was designing these weapons for. They didn't tell me anything besides what they wanted from these weapons. I worked on these designs for two years under the impression that these weapons would be used for our country's protection."

"When did you find out that was false?" Jake asked. Tom took a deep breath. "There was a time during my military days when I studied hacking. I wasn't the best at it, but it was new to me and sparked my interest. This was before I became a weapon engineer, which was my specialty. But I still had some hacking skills. One day, after finishing my work, I was heading back to my room and overheard someone talking about Operation Impact. I don't remember exactly what was said, but I distinctly remember hearing the words 'population reset,' and it concerned me."

Tom stood up and leaned against the wall. "That night, I snuck back into my work area and got on the computer. It took a few hours, but I breached some documents I knew I wasn't supposed to see. It wasn't all there, but there was enough to tell me what was happening. This island I was on had nothing to do with our government or military. I had found myself in the middle of a secret organization that consisted of rogue government and military officials worldwide."

Jake shook his head. "How is this even possible?" he asked. "Why would they drop bombs all over the world and wipe out the population?"

"For control," Tom said. "That was their plan all along. The world was overpopulated, and people were gaining too many rights over the years. Operation Impact was about starting over and developing a new government for the people of the new world. They wanted me to design a bomb that would not only create mass destruction but also release RDA in an attempt to keep any survivors locked away in their shelters. At the time, I thought the idea of RDA was great. I mean, imagine this—drop a nuclear bomb on an enemy country with RDA and still be able to go in and get the country under control without exposing our troops to radiation. The perfect plan, right? But what I didn't know was that their plan the entire time was to build multiple bombs and drop them worldwide."

"How did you get away then?" Jake asked. "You said you were on an island."

"I didn't leave right away," Tom said. "I continued working for them, but with the new information I found, I discreetly changed a few designs here and there. They were subtle changes, but ultimately, it was enough to render the designs useless…or so I thought."

"But how did you get away from them?" Jake asked again.

Tom nodded. "I know you probably don't believe any of this, Jake, but like I said, I continued working for them over the next few months until they were happy with my designs. When all was said and done, they took me back home and thanked me for my service. A few days later, I received a hefty payment in my bank account. I took all the money out and went into hiding."

Jake smirked. "How convenient for you that they

just let you go."

"If anything," Tom replied, "they most likely did it to maintain trust. I mean, I had just designed their dream weapon. Keeping me around while they build multiple bombs may have caused me to question their motives…well, had I not already known what was up."

"So you went on the run, and then what?" Jake asked.

"Not much after that," Tom said. "I built my hideaway house with my bunker. I stocked it up with surveillance equipment to monitor the organization. I eventually started a side business to help people build their shelters. As I told you, I also helped design and build this bunker. But after two years of doing that, I decided that I was moving around too much, so I quit. I met May, and she became pregnant with Nick that same year. We settled down, and I worked at a global newspaper company. Just another way to keep an eye on any breaking global news."

Tom's eyes became distant. "That is until they found me. They knew it was me who made those changes in the design but they somehow worked their way around them during the building process."

Tom sat down again and buried his face in his hands. "They showed up at my office, Jake. I was in another room working on a news project. I went to my office to grab something and I saw them in there going through my things. I knew who they were and left immediately. I did what I could to get away and protect my family, but they got Nick, and May died."

Jake sat down again and rubbed his face. "There is just one thing I don't understand about all of this."

"I can take a wild guess," Tom said. "The president's announcement of the asteroids?"

"Yeah," Jake said.

"That was me," Tom said. "AI technology in a nutshell for ya."

Jake shook his head and stood up. "How do we know you are telling the truth this time?"

"Take me back to my bunker," Tom said, "and I can show you all of it."

"It's gone," Jake said.

Tom's eyes widened. "What do you mean gone?" he asked. "They found it?"

"Yeah," Jake said. "I saw them destroy it." He paused briefly. "They were not wearing suits."

Tom shook his finger at Jake. "See, I told you," he said. "RDA is real. There is no radiation out there. It's all fake."

Emily stood up. "So what does all this mean then?"

she asked. "Where do we go from here?"

Tom looked at Emily. "If you mean going outside, I would advise against it," he said. "We are much safer if we stay down here for now."

"And how much longer would that be?" Jake asked.

"At least until the RDA levels drop," Tom said. "Even though it's harmless, they don't know that the secret is beyond me now. If we go strolling out there without suits and they see us, it won't be a good outcome."

"So we just continue living down here, and we'll be safe?" Emily asked.

"It's the only way," Tom replied. "But the day will come when we will have to leave the bunker, and it will be a different world out there. It will never be the same again."

"But it could be better than we think," Jake said.

"What do you mean?" Tom asked.

Jake thought for a moment and looked at Tom. "You probably saved a lot of people with that message," he said. "As long as there are more survivors out there than these corrupted bastards, it's going to be hard for them to control us."

"That is true," Tom said.

Emily walked over to the door and peeked out. "I

think we should keep this information to ourselves for now," she said. "This might be too big for everyone right now."

"I agree," Jake said. "We can trust Frank though."

"Yes," Emily said. "I'll fill him in later, but as for everyone else, it's too much for them to process right now."

"What about David?" Jake asked.

"Not David," Emily replied. "He's got enough on his plate. Everyone keeps asking him about the levels and when we can go outside. He may end up spilling out information."

Tom stood up. "So we stay in the bunker until further notice, right?"

Emily nodded. "Yes. We stay in the bunker."

Chapter 17

Frank's heart raced as he dashed out of the elevator. The news had reached him through a fellow resident that Jane was in labor. He followed the sound of commotion down the hallway. His breath caught in his throat as he approached the medical room and pushed open the door. There stood Sarah, with relief on her face that he had arrived, and Jane, her brows furrowed in pain, gripping the edges of the bed. Sweat glistened on her forehead as she fought through each contraction.

Frank rushed to her side. "Jane, I'm here. I'm right here with you."

Jane's eyes met his. "Frank," she managed to say between clenched teeth. "I'm so glad you're here."

Frank took Jane's hand in his, gently squeezing it. "You're doing amazing, Jane. Just a little longer, and our baby will be here."

Sarah intervened, her voice calm. "Jane, you're progressing well. Just a few more pushes."

Jane nodded, tightening her grip on Frank's hand. "I can do this."

Time seemed to stand still as the room filled with a symphony of encouragement and labor pains. Finally, after what felt like an eternity, a cry pierced the air.

"It's a boy," Sarah announced. Jane erupted in joyous tears as Frank gazed at their newborn son in awe. Their faces beamed as they held their new arrival to the family.

Frank turned at the sound of a knock on the door and saw Emily standing there with a smile beaming on her face. "Emily!" he exclaimed. "You're here! Come in, come in!"

Emily stepped into the room. "I heard the good news and had to come down here. Congratulations! He looks so adorable!"

"Thank you, Emily," Jane said.

Emily approached the bed, her excitement bubbling

over. "He will bring so much love and happiness into your lives. I can already see it. What's his name?"

"This is our little Benjamin," Jane said

Emily's face lit up. "Benjamin. It's a perfect name for such a handsome little boy."

"Thank you for being here, Emily," Frank said.

"I wouldn't have missed it for the world," Emily replied. She turned to Jane. "You must be exhausted. I'll leave you to get some rest. I have a few things I need to get back to."

Jane smiled. "Thanks for the visit, Emily. I do need to get some rest."

Emily excused herself from the room. She returned to her office, where she found Tom waiting for her.

"Emily, we need to talk," he said.

"What's on your mind," Emily replied.

Tom paced the room before sitting down. "Did Jake talk to you about our plans?"

"Plans?" Emily asked. "What plans are you talking about?"

Tom shook his head. "I'll wait for him to get here. He should be on his way now."

"Tom…" Emily started.

"No," Tom said. "I won't discuss this without him."

Before Emily could respond, Jake stepped into the

office. He looked at Tom and then at Emily, who had a worried look on her face.

"Wait, Tom, did you tell Emily about what we talked about?" Jake asked.

Tom shook his head. "No, I haven't told her yet. I thought it was best to wait for you."

"What is it, Jake?" Emily asked. "What haven't you told me?"

Jake took Emily's hand. "Tom and I have been discussing the possibility of going out and gathering more information on what Compton and his men are up to."

Emily's eyes widened. "Jake, that's a horrible idea," she said. "These people are dangerous. I mean, look what they did to the world."

Jake nodded. "I understand, Emily. But if we don't take action, we may remain in the dark forever. We owe it to ourselves and everyone in this bunker to find out what they are planning to do next."

Emily shook her head. "And how do you suppose you do that?" she asked. "You can't just wander around out there. What if they catch you?"

"You're right, Emily," Tom said. "We can't let our desire for answers overshadow the importance of safety. Which is why I have a plan."

"What plan is that, Tom?" Emily asked.

Tom smiled. "I have another bunker to spy on them from."

Jake looked at Tom with confusion. "Wait a minute now" he said. "You didn't say anything about another bunker."

"I know," Tom said. "But I do. I'm on the run from an island full of lunatic terrorists who bombed the entire world. Of course I'm going to have more than one bunker to hide from them."

"When were you going to reveal this to us?" Emily asked.

"Well," Tom said. "Apparently, I was going to reveal it now."

"You're a funny guy," Jake said.

Tom laughed. "Sarcasm, I like it."

"So what's this plan you have?" Jake asked.

"Easy enough," Tom said. "We go to my other bunker and gather all the information we can get our hands on. They won't stay on that island forever. In fact, the RDA levels are already dropping, and they are bound to come out at any moment to scout for emerging survivors. We can't be sitting ducks down here when they do. We need to be able to fight back when the time comes."

Jake looked into Emily's eyes. "He's right," he said. "We have been down here for too long. If we ever want a chance to get out of here, we need to ensure that it will be safe to do so without walking into another threat."

Emily sighed. "Jake, I share your hope for freedom; I really do. I want out of here just as much as the next person. But you need to think about the risks involved in doing something like this."

Jake turned to Tom. "You go ahead; I need to talk to Emily for a moment."

"Sure thing, Jake," Tom replied, giving them a nod before stepping out of the room.

As the door closed behind Tom, Emily fell into Jake's embrace. "I hope you know what you're doing, Jake," she whispered. "I can't help but be scared for your safety."

Jake held Emily tightly. "I understand your worries, Em. But you know I've been out there before. This time, I'll be going with the knowledge of what is happening, and I'll know what to expect."

Emily looked into his eyes. "I know, Jake," she said. "I just don't want to lose you."

Jake leaned in and kissed her. With a final glance, he pulled away from her and headed toward the door.

As he stepped out, he saw Tom waiting patiently. Jake gave him a nod, and they both started walking down the hallway. It was time to figure out how to put a stop to this once and for all.

Chapter 18

Frank raised his ceramic coffee cup to his lips, taking a measured sip of the steaming brew. The warm, rich aroma filled the air as he looked at Emily with concern.

"I think it's finally time to call that meeting," he said. "People have been talking and noticing that Jake and Tom have been disappearing a lot over the last few months."

"I know," she replied. "I'm just trying to devise a way to tell them without causing panic."

Frank nodded. "Jake and Tom are out today, aren't they?"

Emily confirmed with a nod. "Yes, they should be back later tonight."

Frank took another sip and set his cup down. "I think it's best to tell them before they return. You know I'm right here by your side. Daniel and Rob are with us, too."

Emily appreciated the support, but Jake had implored her to hold off on the meeting, urging her to wait until he and Tom could come up with a final plan to put a stop to this madness. Yet, there was no guarantee that any of their expeditions outside the bunker would yield the answers they so desperately sought. The risks involved in revealing their actions might ultimately put the entire community in danger, exposing them to the forces that had laid waste to civilization.

But deep in her heart, Emily knew that hope was the fragile lifeline that kept them all going. Regardless of the outcome, the people needed to hear the truth. It was the only way to maintain a sense of purpose amid the stark reality of life underground. They deserved to know why they were down here.

"You're right," Emily said. "I will call that meeting now."

* * *

As they hiked through the woods, Jake couldn't help but wonder about their destination. He and Tom had spent the last few months working tirelessly, gathering information on the island. The people behind Operation Impact were starting to move, and time was running out. But today was different. Instead of going to Tom's bunker, Jake was following him blindly through the woods.

He could feel the beads of sweat trickling down his brow. Although it felt amazing to be outside without wearing a radiation suit, hours of walking had left him drenched as if he was still wearing one.

Tom glanced over his shoulder. "I believe it's time for a well-earned break."

Jake came to a halt. "Another break? Are you ever going to tell me where we're going?"

Tom turned to Jake with a smile. "It's time for you to meet my other contact."

Jake shot Tom a look. "Contact?"

"I've got an associate out here," Tom explained. "Someone I used to work with who shares our discontent with Operation Impact. You can trust him."

Jake shook his head in disbelief. "Geez, Tom, how

179

many secrets have you been keeping from us?"

"Likely no more secrets than you've got stored away from the people in that bunker of yours."

Jake met Tom's gaze with a stern look. "It's been months, Tom. I trust you now. Any more surprises you're keeping?"

Tom took a moment to consider his response. "Well," he began, "I used the bunker's radio to stay in contact with him."

"I don't know what to make of you anymore," Jake muttered. "Are you certain we can trust him?"

"There's every reason to trust him," Tom said. "He's as committed to dismantling this madness as we are."

"How much farther do we have to go?" Jake asked.

"We're actually here now," Tom replied. "I just needed to catch my breath first." He knelt down and grabbed a handful of leaves.

Jake was confused at first but quickly realized that Tom had picked up a camouflage netting which revealed a steel door set into the earth. With a rhythmic knock, Tom patiently waited. A few seconds later, a latch unlocked, and the door slowly opened.

"Hey, Tom," a voice called from the depths below.

Jake's gaze shifted to the man emerging from the hidden chamber.

"You must be Jake," he declared with a friendly grin. "I've heard quite a bit about you."

Jake's response carried a hint of skepticism as he locked eyes with Tom. "I'm afraid I can't share the same sentiment."

"Come on, Jake," Tom urged. "This is Carl. Let's move inside where it's safer, and we can fill you in on much more."

Carl chimed in. "Welcome to my bunker, Jake. Seems like we all got one nowadays."

As he descended the concrete stairs, Jake noticed an imposing steel door, much like the one he had seen in Tom's shelter. "Let me guess," he said.

Tom held his grin. "You've guessed it right. I designed this one as well."

Carl entered the key code and swung open the door, revealing a space reminiscent of Tom's sanctuary. Tables lined the walls, adorned with monitors and equipment.

"So, what's the story?" Jake asked. "Seems like you got a well-organized operation going on down here."

"We understand you can fly a helicopter, correct?" Carl asked.

Jake looked confused. "How did you know that?" he said, turning to Tom.

Tom grabbed a newspaper and tossed it on a table next to Jake.

Jake picked it up and noticed it was the same newspaper article that he had seen at Tom's bunker. The detailed photo showed the scene at the bunker gate that day. Among the crowd, he could see himself standing guard as the chaos unfolded. Upon closer look, he could see his wings displayed on his uniform.

Jake couldn't help but chuckle. "You are quite the stalker, ya know," he said as he tossed the paper back at Tom.

Tom laughed. "Hey, what can I say? It's my specialty to be nosy nowadays."

"What does this mean?" Jake asked. "Why do you need me to fly a helicopter?"

"Because…" Tom said, his face suddenly becoming serious, "We are going to the island."

* * *

Emily took a deep breath and began to speak. "Everyone," her voice cut through the air, drawing the attention of the assembled crowd. She paused briefly and looked at Frank beside her.

"It's okay," Frank reassured. "I'm right here."

Emily turned her attention back to the faces before her. "I stand before you with an important announcement. As we've all endured, our existence has been confined within this bunker for nearly two years. The events of that fateful day took a toll on each of us, but here we are, survivors. That, above all, is what matters. Our strength has carried us this far, and I implore each of you to hold onto that truth."

A ripple of nods and murmurs of agreement echoed through the crowd.

She continued. "But beneath the surface of our survival, there's a layer of our story that goes beyond what we initially understood. New revelations have come to light, thanks to our newest member, Tom. These are insights that none of us could have imagined, and you all deserve to know the truth."

With one final deep breath, Emily broke the news. "Asteroids did not hit the earth. They were bombs."

Chapter 19

"What do you mean we're going to the island?" Jake asked. "That place has to be crawling with security. There's no way we can set foot there without getting caught."

Carl settled into a worn chair and started typing on the keyboard in front of him. "Not exactly," he said. "Come check this out."

Intrigued, Jake approached the computer, where Carl's fingers continued dancing across the keys. Finally, he leaned back in his chair. "Look at this, Jake."

Jake's eyes widened as he gazed at the monitor. "Is that what I think it is?" he asked.

"Yep," Carl replied. "That's satellite images of the island. We've been watching them."

A look of concern etched across Jake's face. "They can't track this, can they?"

"They most definitely can," Carl said. "but I'm spoofing the coordinates. If they send their goons to find it, they'll be searching 1000 miles away."

A daring grin played on Jake's lips. "As risky as it sounds, it's also genius."

Tom chuckled, "That's Carl for you. A true genius."

Jake smiled. "For a bunch of corrupted government officials, you'd think they would have beefed up the security," he remarked.

Tom responded, "Well, they didn't anticipate someone like me stepping in to foil their plans. As far as they were concerned, they were supposed to be the sole survivors in this lonely world. Thanks to me, we now have a world full of pissed-off survivors. People who have lost loved ones."

"How many bunkers have you had contact with since the bombs were dropped?" Jake asked.

"Enough to get the word out," he replied. "I contact them, and they reach out to other bunkers. The information spreads like wildfire. By the way, has Emily made the announcement yet?"

"As far as I know, she hasn't," Jake replied. "I would hope that she waits until we get back. There's no telling how the people will react."

Tom nodded. "I'm sure they would understand."

"I think it's time to get down to business," Carl said. "So Jake, are you interested in the plan?"

Jake leaned against the wall, crossing his arms. He fell into a deep thought before finally responding. "I guess I don't really have a choice. What's the plan?"

Tom leaned in. "There's a cluster of smaller islands a few miles from the main one," he said. "We'll take a helicopter under the radar, then switch to a raft to reach the main island."

Jake processed this, his mind spinning with the details. "So, we'll need to bring a raft on the helicopter," he mused. As ridiculous as it sounded, it wasn't impossible.

Tom gave a nod. "Exactly. No luxurious yachts for us—just a modest raft with a small motor. Once we're near the island, we'll paddle the rest of the way."

"Rub a dub dub, three men in a tub," Jake said flatly.

Tom glanced at Jake, then at Carl, then back to Jake. Suddenly, they all burst into laughter. It was the most laughter any of them have had in such a long time.

Jake wiped tears from his eyes and added, "But seriously, if these government goons don't catch us, the sharks might."

Tom's grin widened. "You're a soldier, aren't you, Jake?"

"Yeah, but I'm more accustomed to the solid ground than the open sea," Jake admitted.

Tom shrugged, dismissing Jake's concerns with a wave of his hand. "It's all the same," he remarked casually. "Whether you meet your end on land or at sea, the outcome remains unchanged."

"I suppose so," Jake conceded. "Though, if given the choice, I'd prefer to avoid meeting my end altogether. But if this is the only way to stop them, count me in."

"Good man," Carl said. "Once we arrive, our next challenge will be infiltrating the compound."

"And what's your strategy for pulling that off?" Jake asked.

Tom's demeanor remained resolute. "Let me paint you a picture," he began. "I'm a man with nothing left to lose. They ripped my family away from me and left me with no choice but to flee. But if I retain even a shred of value to them, they'll allow me entry."

"You're playing a dangerous game, Tom," Jake

cautioned. "Walking into the lion's den like that, you're risking your life. What if they shoot you on sight?"

"Perhaps," he said. "But I'm counting on the possibility that they won't. I'm hoping for a slim chance to make a difference, to strike back at the heart of their operation."

Jake's expression softened. "And what about us? What's our role in this while you're inside?"

Tom's gaze remained steady. "While I'm in there, I'll cause a distraction to draw all the guards to my location. You'll secure one of their helicopters for our escape. Meanwhile, Carl will locate the remaining bombs and set them to detonate on a timer."

Jake shook his head. "How do you know they didn't drop all of the bombs?"

Carl pointed to the sattelite images. "They've been moving them around the compound," he said. "Possibly preparing them for another strike if needed."

A weary smile tugged at Jake's lips. "I see where this is heading. But I'll let you have the pleasure of saying it yourself."

"That's right," Tom declared, a fire burning in his eyes. "We're going to blow them up just like they blew us up."

Chapter 20

Emily's gaze swept across the sea of faces. Anticipation gripped her as she awaited their reaction to the bombshell she had just dropped. The tension hung thick in the air.

"Emily, how could you keep this from us?" a voice broke the stillness.

The crowd shifted, faces reflecting anger and betrayal. Murmurs of discontent rippled through the crowd.

"Calm down, everyone!" Frank raised his hands. "Let's not turn on each other."

"I thought I was doing the right thing," Emily said,

her voice trembling. "I didn't want to give any of you false hopes until I had enough information."

"False hopes?" Another voice cut through the air. "What hopes do we have at all if you're going to keep something like this from us?"

Frank stepped forward, trying to refocus the group. "Listen, we need to understand what's really going on. Emily is still our leader, and she deserves a chance to explain."

The crowd remained tense, but Frank's calm demeanor seemed to help.

"Please, let me explain," Emily urged. "I should have told you the truth from the beginning."

A hush fell over the crowd, their expressions shifting.

"Let's go back to the start," she continued. "It all traces back to when Jake first contacted Tom over the radio."

* * *

Jake, Tom, and Carl trekked through the woods toward the bunker to finalize their plans to go to the island. Uncertainty crept into Jake's mind. He couldn't help but wonder if they were walking into a suicide mission.

"Are we ready for this?" Jake asked, breaking the heavy silence.

Tom glanced back. "Do we have a choice? We've come this far, Jake. We have to see it through."

Carl nodded in agreement, but Jake could see the flicker of doubt in his eyes.

"What if we're not enough?" Jake asked.

Tom's eyes hardened with resolve. "Then we go down fighting. Besides, we have a better chance of getting in undetected if we keep our numbers low."

Carl placed a hand on Jake's shoulder. "I'm not going to lie," he said. "Doubt is trying to creep its way into my head, too. But we can do this. We have to—for the chance to rebuild."

They walked in silence until they finally reached the bunker. Jake paused, giving Tom one last look before reaching down to open the hatch.

"We're ready for this," Tom said quietly.

"Let's finish this," Jake replied.

With a decisive pull, he opened the hatch, and they descended into the bunker.

Each pair of eyes was locked on Emily, hanging on every word as she concluded her story. She had expected more anger to flare up again for keeping the truth from them for so long. Yet, she saw understanding, even compassion. They weren't just a group of survivors but a community bound together by shared hardship and trust.

"I know I've kept a lot from you," Emily said. "Every decision I made was with your best interests at heart. I was scared of what was out there and what the future held. I thought I was protecting you all from that burden by carrying it all on myself."

"You did what you thought was right," Frank said softly. "And we're still here because of you."

"We're all scared," one voice said from the back. "But we trust you."

Another voice said, "Yeah, we've made it this far, thanks to you."

"Thank you," Emily said, her voice thick with emotion.

Suddenly, a high-pitched screech pierced the air, snapping everyone's attention toward the source of the sound.

"Jake's back!" Lily screamed, her voice filled with excitement as she bolted away from the crowd.

Jake's face lit up with a genuine smile as he dropped to his knees to meet Lily's hug. "Hey, Lily," he said softly. Are you holding down the fort?"

"Sure am," Lily replied.

Jake chuckled, ruffling her hair gently. "Well, keep it up."

Emily, unable to contain her emotions any longer, made her way through the crowd toward Jake. She threw her arms around him, pulling him into a tight hug. "I missed you so much," she whispered. "I was so worried."

Jake returned the hug, his hand gently caressing her back. "I missed you too, Emily," he said. Emily pulled back slightly, looking into his eyes before kissing him softly.

Frank, standing quietly nearby, cleared his throat and broke the moment. "Um...Sorry to interrupt, but it looks like you've brought a new friend with you?" He gestured toward Carl.

Jake turned and stepped back, realizing he had yet to introduce their newcomer. "Oh, right. My bad," he said, a bit sheepishly. "Frank, Emily, this is Carl. He's with Tom. Don't worry, he's cool."

"Nice to meet you, Carl," Emily said, extending her hand. "Any friend of Tom's is welcome here."

Carl shook her hand. "Thanks."

Frank stepped forward. "Welcome, Carl. If Jake and Tom vouch for you, that's good enough for me." He glanced at Jake, then back at Carl. "We've all been through a lot, and trust is hard-earned these days."

"You got that right," Jake said, smirking toward Tom.

Tom raised an eyebrow. "Hey, I had reasons to be hesitant before, but look at me now. Trustworthy as can be."

Jake chuckled. "I don't know about that. I'm sure there are a few more secrets hiding in that noggin of yours."

Tom grinned. "Wouldn't you like to know?"

"Come on now," Emily said. "I'm sure we have a lot to talk about."

"Oh, you bet we do," Tom replied

Emily's eyes flicked to Jake, her concern deepening.

"Emily," Jake said, "just a heads-up, you won't like it, but we have a plan. Let's go talk."

Jake turned to Lily, who was standing by patiently, her young face bright with curiosity. "Lily, why don't you pick out a game for us to play later tonight?"

Lily's eyes widened with excitement. "Ok, Jake!" she exclaimed. "I'll be sure to pick a good one."

"Awesome," Jake replied. He turned back to Emily. "Alright, let's go get this over with."

Chapter 21

"You can't be serious," Emily said. She paced back and forth in the cramped office. "You can't do that, Jake, you'll be killed. You'll all be killed."

Jake stood firm. "It's a risk," he admitted "But it's a risk that could change everything. This could be how it all ends."

Emily stopped mid-step, her eyes locking onto his. "I don't care about that, Jake. I care about you. I won't lose you."

Jake took a step forward, reaching out to gently take her hand. He could feel the tremor in her fingers.

"Emily, I don't want to lose you either," he said softly. "But if we don't do this…" He paused, struggling to find the right words. "If we don't do this, we might lose everything we've been fighting for."

Carl spoke up. "They will eventually find us. And when they do, you'll lose not only Jake but everyone in this bunker you care about. We can't just sit here and wait for them to come to us."

Emily's gaze shifted to Carl, her eyes searching his face for any sign of doubt. "How do you know that for sure?" she challenged.

"Carl's right," Tom said. "They'll do whatever it takes to rebuild this world on their terms. No freedom, no future, just their rules. If we don't fight back now, we might never get another chance."

"But there has to be another way," she pleaded, her voice cracking. "There has to be something else we can do."

Frank suddenly stepped forward. "I'm going with you," he declared.

Jake turned to him, surprised by the sudden outburst. "Frank, you don't have to."

"I'm going," Frank insisted.

"Frank, no," Emily said, her voice gentle but firm. "You can't go. You have to stay here for Jane. For Lily and Benjamin."

"She's right, Frank," Jake said. "You have a family that needs you here. You're their rock. They depend on you. And we need you here, too. Emily will need your help running this place while we're gone."

Frank's shoulders slumped in defeat, and he nodded reluctantly. "You're right," he said quietly.

Emily turned back to Jake, her eyes glistening with tears that she was fighting hard to hold back. She reached out, cupping his face in her hands, her touch trembling. "Just promise me you'll come back," she whispered.

"I promise I'll do everything I can to come back to you," he said softly.

Tom cleared his throat, drawing everyone's attention back to reality. "We need to finalize our plans," he said. "We can't afford to waste any more time."

Emily wiped her eyes. "Alright," she said. "Let's do this. For our future."

The group gathered around the small table in the center of the room, their voices overlapping as they discussed the plan's details. Emily stood by, listening to them strategize.

"We need to leave at dawn," Tom said. "Get some rest. We move out in the morning."

They all got up from the table, and Emily pulled Jake aside.

Jake sensed another resistance from Emily and quickly intervened. "We'll be careful," Jake assured her. "I need you to stay strong."

She nodded as she teared up again. "Just…come back to me, Jake."

Chapter 22

Emily's eyes snapped open, and she instinctively reached over to Jake's side of the bed, but it was empty. The early morning darkness lingered in the room, filling it with an unsettling stillness.

She got up and rubbed her eyes before going to the kitchen. When she walked in, Frank was already brewing the coffee. He looked up as she entered and nodded in greeting.

"Morning," he said quietly.

"Morning," she replied, her voice strained. She looked around, then asked, "Did you see them off?"

Frank nodded. "Yeah, I saw them leave a little while ago."

Emily's heart sank further. She had hoped she would have one last chance to say goodbye, but Jake had chosen to slip away quietly. She stood there, not knowing what to say next, the weight of the situation pressing down on her.

Frank reached into his pocket and pulled out something small, holding it out to her. "Jake wanted you to have this," he said.

Emily frowned, taking the object from him. It was Jake's dog tags. She stared at them, her mind struggling to process what this meant.

"He told me to tell you not to worry about him," Frank continued, "and that he will see you again soon."

Emily gripped the tags tightly. She wanted to cry but held it back, forcing herself to stay strong.

"Did he say anything else?" she asked.

Frank shook his head. "Just that he didn't want to wake you. He thought it would be easier that way."

Emily nodded, though she felt anything but at ease. She turned the tags over, her thumb tracing the engraved letters. It was a small, tangible piece of Jake to hold onto while he was gone.

"I'm scared, Frank," she admitted after a moment.

"What if he doesn't come back?"

Frank placed a hand on her shoulder. "No more of that," he said firmly. "You promised Jake you would be strong."

Emily nodded, knowing he was right. "Thanks, Frank. I appreciate it."

"You're tougher than you think, Emily," Frank replied. "Now, let's get some of that coffee."

* * *

Tom led the way through the dense woods, his steps cautious against the early morning chill. The forest was draped in a thick layer of fog, giving their surroundings an eerie, dreamlike quality. Jake and Carl followed closely, their breaths forming small clouds in the frigid air. The silence between them was heavy; each one lost in their own thoughts as they pushed forward.

Suddenly, the sharp crack of gunfire broke the stillness. All three men dropped to the ground instinctively, their hearts pounding as they scanned the area. Tom motioned for them to take cover in the nearby bushes. They scrambled to hide, hunkering down as they strained to listen.

"Where did that come from?" Jake whispered.

Tom didn't answer, holding up a hand to keep them silent. They could hear footsteps now—two sets, coming closer, crunching through the underbrush.

"Stay down," Tom whispered. "Let them pass."

They peered through the leaves as two men emerged from the fog, their silhouettes dark against the misty gray. They were moving cautiously, their eyes scanning the surroundings as they muttered to each other. Tom's grip tightened on the knife at his belt.

Jake leaned close. "We can't let them find the bunker. We need to take them out."

Tom nodded in agreement and then turned to Carl, who was already gripping his rifle. "Cover us," Tom instructed. "Jake and I will handle them quietly."

Carl gave a nod, positioning himself to get a clear shot if things went south. Tom and Jake began to move, creeping through the brush.

The two enemy men continued their search, unaware of the danger stalking them from behind. Jake's pulse raced as they closed the distance. Tom gave the green light, and they struck. Tom grabbed the first man from behind, clamping a hand over his mouth and twisting his neck with a sharp, precise motion. The man went limp, his body dropping to the ground. At the exact moment, Jake took down the second man, his movements equally swift and lethal.

They stood over the bodies for a few seconds, breathing heavily as the fog swirled around them. Tom wiped his brow, glancing at Jake.

"Nice work," Jake muttered, his voice still low. "But we need to move. Quickly."

Tom nodded, gesturing for Carl to join them. Together, they dragged the bodies into the underbrush, covering them with leaves and branches in a hasty attempt to hide the evidence.

"Let's get to the helicopter," Tom urged. "We don't have much time."

They resumed their trek through the woods, moving with renewed speed. After what felt like an eternity, the forest began to thin, and the silhouette of the helicopter finally emerged from the fog. Compton's men had landed here a few weeks ago and were scouting the area. Carl had taken it upon himself to dispatch them, securing the helicopter for their mission.

Jake approached the helicopter. He ran his hands over the cold metal, his eyes narrowing as he inspected it. "I haven't flown in years," he said.

"Well, I hope you didn't forget how," Tom joked.

Carl looked around before turning to Jake. "Those two men we just took out must have been looking for their scouts."

Jake nodded, "I wouldn't doubt it."

They climbed into the helicopter. Jake took the pilot's seat and began pushing buttons and flipping switches as if he had been flying every day for the last two years. The rotors slowly spun to life, the hum of the aircraft cutting through the morning fog as it lifted off the ground.

The helicopter soared over the coastline, the dense forest on one side and the open sea on the other. Jake guided the aircraft toward their destination several miles from the main island housing the facility responsible for Operation Impact.

The helicopter touched down on the beach, and Jake quickly cut the engines. They jumped out, and Tom opened the cargo area. He pulled out the quick-deploy raft they would be using for the next chapter of their journey. He tossed it on the ground, reached back into the cargo, and pulled out a small outboard motor.

"I hope this thing works," Tom said. "We leave tonight."

They set up a small camp in a wooded area just off the beach; a fire crackled softly as the evening chill set in. The warmth was welcome, but it did little to ease the tension. They gathered around the fire, the flames casting long shadows on their faces as they discussed the final details of their plan.

"This is it," Carl said. "We're on the brink of a major operation."

Tom nodded, his eyes reflecting the firelight. "We're doing this for a reason," he said quietly. "For everyone we've lost, and for everyone we're still fighting to protect."

Jake looked up to the sky, his heart feeling heavy as the sun dipped below the horizon. The night was closing in, bringing with it the moment they had been preparing for.

"Alright," Tom said, breaking the silence over them. "Let's do this."

They gathered their things, moving quietly. Jake doused the fire, leaving only the faint smell of smoke lingering in the air. Tom dragged the raft down to the edge of the water and yanked the string. The raft quickly inflated, and Tom attached the motor. They climbed aboard, and with a gentle push, they began to drift away from the shore.

Tom started the engine with a low rumble that cut through the silence. "We'll run the engine until we're a mile from the island," he said. "Then we'll paddle in to avoid detection."

Jake leaned back against the side of the raft, the salty sea breeze brushing against his face. His mind drifted to Emily, her face vivid in his memory, the only light in the dark corners of his thoughts. He could almost feel her hand in his, hearing her voice telling him to return safely. The idea of not making it back to her was unbearable.

He closed his eyes briefly, praying silently to whatever force might be listening. A single tear escaped, sliding down his cheek before he could stop it. He quickly wiped it away, clearing his throat as he forced himself to focus on their mission.

As they sailed into the night, the shoreline faded from view, swallowed by the darkness. Ahead of them, only the ocean remained and beyond that, the island.

* * *

Emily finally sat down in her office. It had been a long, busy day filled with anything she could get her hands on to take her mind off of Jake's absence. She had visited Jane to help out with the baby, taken a stroll through the gardens with Robert, and even managed to get through a movie with Lily.

But now that the day was over, everyone had

abandoned her to their rooms for the night. The worrying thoughts she had fought so hard to suppress were starting to flood her head again. She heard footsteps in the hall, and she looked up just as Frank entered through the door.

"Hey," he said gently. "I wanted to check up on you before I went to bed. Are you doing alright?"

Emily summoned a smile that didn't quite reach her eyes. "Yeah, just…thinking," she replied.

Frank moved closer, pulling out the chair across from her and settling himself in. "Thinking about Jake?"

"I can't stop," she replied.

"It's good to think about him," Frank said. "Think about him all you want. But it's not good to constantly worry yourself. It's not healthy."

Emily nodded. "I was somehow able to get through most of the day worry-free," she said.

Frank smiled. "Well, there you go. I knew you could do it. I'm proud of you."

"I love him," she blurted out. She almost couldn't believe she actually said that out loud.

Frank blinked a few times, unsure of what to say.

"I mean…" Emily started, but it was too late. It was out now. "I mean, I love him, but…what if he doesn't feel the same way?"

Frank shook his head, a look of disbelief on his face. "Emily, I've seen you two together. There's something real there. It's clear as day."

She looked down. "So...you don't think I'm fooling myself?"

"In my honest opinion," Frank said, "I'd say you'd be fooling yourself to think he doesn't love you because, guess what, Emily...he does."

She took a long breath as if a weight had been lifted off her chest. "I just don't want to lose him before I tell him," she said quietly.

"You won't," Frank assured her. "When he's back, say everything you need to say."

Emily rose from the table, stretching her legs. "I should try to get some rest," she murmured, glancing at the clock. "It's been a long day."

"Get some sleep," Frank said, rising with her.

"Thank you, Frank," she replied. "I really appreciate everything."

She returned to her room and climbed into bed, the darkness settling around her like a comforting blanket. Closing her eyes, she felt her heart beating steadily, carrying a quiet but fierce confession that filled the silence of the night.

"I love you, Jake," she whispered, letting the words linger and fill the quiet room with a soft, unbreakable promise.

Chapter 23

The raft cut quietly through the still water, the rhythmic hum of the motor the only sound against the backdrop of the night. The moonlight rippled across the surface of the sea, casting a faint glow stretching endlessly around them. Jake sat, staring at the vast, empty horizon, the distant island looming ahead like a shadowed promise.

Tom's eyes were locked forward as he steered them on their course. Carl sat beside Jake, gripping the edge of the raft as if it would somehow anchor him. The night air was cold and sharp, the wind tugging at their clothes, but Jake hardly noticed. His mind was far away, back at the bunker, back with Emily.

It wasn't the first time she'd crossed his thoughts since they'd set off, but the closer they got to the island, the heavier the weight of her absence became. He could see her face clearly in his mind: the way her brow furrowed when she was worried, the soft, hopeful smile she gave him even when things were bleak. That smile haunted him now, more than ever.

Carl noticed the far-away look in Jake's eyes and nudged him with an elbow. "You're thinking about her, aren't you?"

Jake blinked and glanced at Carl, his grip tightening around the oar beside him. "Yeah. Can't help it."

Carl smiled knowingly, though there was little humor in it. "I get it, man. We all left people behind. It doesn't make this any easier."

Jake nodded silently, turning his gaze back toward the horizon. The island was growing more extensive now, and the jagged cliffs that lined the shore became more defined as they approached. The weight in his chest grew heavier with every mile they traveled.

"I just hope we make it back," Jake muttered, almost to himself.

"We will," Carl said. "We've got too much riding on this not to."

Jake forced a smile, but the doubt still gnawed at him. He had made promises—to Emily, to himself—but promises felt fragile out here, lost in the endless sea and darkness. He couldn't shake the feeling that something was about to go wrong, that they were walking into something bigger than any of them realized.

Tom suddenly cut the motor, the sound dying into the quiet rush of the water around them. He grabbed an oar and motioned for the others to do the same.

"From here, we row," he said in a low voice. "No more noise. We don't want to alert anyone."

Jake dipped his oar into the water as Carl did the same. Together, they began to row in sync, their strokes slow and deliberate, barely making a sound as they pushed the raft forward. The silence of the night seemed to deepen around them, and the occasional splash of the oars was the only thing breaking the stillness.

After several long minutes, Carl's voice came in a whisper. "You think they're waiting for us?"

Tom didn't answer right away. He kept his focus ahead, watching the island as they inched closer.

"Could be," he finally said. "But we stick to the plan. Get in, do what we came for, and get out."

Carl grunted, clearly not reassured by Tom's calm

demeanor. "Right."

Jake glanced at Carl, catching the nervousness in his voice. "Stick with it, Carl. We're almost there. Just focus."

Carl sighed, gripping his oar tighter. "I'm focused, man. I'm just saying—this feels like we're heading into something we can't control. I hate that feeling."

"You're not wrong," Jake admitted, though he tried to keep his voice steady. "But we don't have a choice."

Carl shook his head, muttering under his breath. "No choice. Right."

They rowed in silence for what felt like hours, though it was only a matter of minutes. The island was so close now that Jake could make out the rocky shoreline and the dense forest that stood like a wall just beyond it. The cliffs loomed above them, casting deep shadows over the beach. The air grew colder, and the faint sound of the waves crashed against the rocks.

Tom was the first to speak again. "We're almost there. When we hit the shore, we move fast. Stay quiet. No mistakes."

Carl let out a breath. "No mistakes," he echoed.

Tom raised his hand as they neared the shore, signaling them to slow their strokes. The raft drifted in the last few feet, scraping softly against the sand. The sound was barely audible over the waves' distant crash, but it felt deafening to Jake. His pulse quickened. They had made it.

Tom stood up, his movements slow as he stepped out of the raft and onto the sand. He glanced back at Jake and Carl, motioning for them to follow. "Come on. We move now," he whispered.

Jake's legs were shaky as he stood. His muscles ached from rowing, but he ignored the discomfort, forcing himself to focus. There was no time for weakness now. He stepped out of the raft, his boots sinking into the wet sand as he scanned the shoreline. The island felt empty. Too quiet. Too still.

Carl followed, his movements more hesitant, his eyes wide as he looked around. "This place gives me the creeps," he muttered.

Tom shot him a look. "Stay focused. We're not out of the woods yet."

Carl swallowed hard and nodded, though his hands still trembled slightly as he adjusted the strap of his pack. "Right. Focused. Got it."

The three of them moved quickly, their steps silent as they made their way off the beach and toward the cover of the trees. Jake's heart raced in his chest, his senses on high alert as they left the raft behind.

Tom led the way, his eyes scanning the treeline. He was calm and controlled, but Jake knew him well enough to see the tension in his posture. He could feel it, too—the weight of the unknown hanging over them like a storm cloud. As they reached the forest's edge, Jake glanced back at the raft, now barely visible in the shadows.

Tom stopped just inside the cover of the trees, his hand raised in a silent signal for them to halt. He crouched low, peering through the darkness ahead, his eyes narrowed in concentration. Jake and Carl followed suit, crouching beside him, their breaths shallow in the still night air.

In a clearing ahead, two guards engaged in lighthearted banter, unaware of the three intruders who had just set foot on their island.

"Alright," Tom said, determination blazing in his eyes. "I'm going in. Once I'm inside, you know what to do."

"Just be careful," Jake replied, a note of concern threading through his voice.

Taking a deep breath, Tom rose and stepped toward the guards. As he approached, the guards snapped to attention, weapons trained on him.

"Who are you?" one demanded.

Tom stopped, his expression steady. "Tell that old bastard General Compton that Tom is back."

Chapter 24

The smell of saltwater mixed with mildew lingered in the air as Tom sat, stiff and on edge, in the worn, uncomfortable wooden chair. General Compton's office had mainly stayed the same since Tom had last been there. The walls were lined with military regalia and photographs from years past, reminders of the general's long-standing career. A large, imposing desk sat between them, cluttered with documents and reports that hadn't been touched in days. The air was damp and heavy with the oppressive heat that clung to every corner of the room. The overhead fan creaked rhythmically but did little to offer relief.

General Compton loomed over the desk, his sharp, cold eyes fixed on Tom, scrutinizing him from across the room. Tom could feel the weight of the general's gaze like a predator sizing up prey. Compton's fingers drummed lightly on the desk, the steady tap-tap-tap reverberating in the small space, heightening the tension. Tom's heart raced in his chest, but he kept his expression neutral. He couldn't afford to give anything away.

"So," Compton's voice was low. "You just decided to come back, did you? After all this time?"

Tom didn't move. He met Compton's gaze with a measured, resigned look of a beaten man. Inside, however, his mind raced. He had rehearsed this moment a thousand times in his head.

"I'm tired, Compton," Tom finally said, his voice carrying a weariness that was all too real. "I've lost everything. My family, my home, my future. There's nothing left for me out there. I spent years running from you, from all of this," he gestured vaguely around the office. "But I'm done running."

Compton leaned forward, elbows resting on the desk. The dim light overhead shadowed his face, but his eyes glittered with suspicion.

"And I'm supposed to believe that?" Compton's

voice dripped with disbelief. "That after everything—after all the trouble you've caused me—you're just giving up?"

Tom shrugged, but his movements were slow. "Believe what you want," he replied, his tone flat. "But I've got nothing left to fight for. No one left to protect." He let his gaze fall to the floor as if he couldn't bear to meet the general's eyes. "I'm just tired of running."

For a long moment, Compton said nothing. The silence hung heavy between them, broken only by the faint hum of the fan overhead. Tom could feel the sweat on the back of his neck, the heat pressing down on him. He needed to sell this performance. It was a delicate balance. He needed to seem defeated enough to gain Compton's trust but not so weak that he appeared useless.

Compton finally broke the silence. "You know, Tom, you jeopardized my entire operation by changing those designs. You caused a delay that lasted years. Why should I trust you now, Tom?" His eyes narrowed as if trying to peel back the layers of Tom's façade. "You betrayed us—what makes this time different?"

Tom leaned forward, resting his elbows on his knees, his fingers laced together. He let out a heavy sigh, shaking his head. "I'm not asking you to trust me," he said. "Hell, I wouldn't trust me either. But look around, Compton. The world is over, and there's nothing left to do but move forward. I'd rather help rebuild than run for the rest of my life. You know I have skills, Compton. You know that you need me. Who's going to pass on those skills to others in the future?"

The general studied him for what felt like an eternity, his expression unreadable. Finally, he stood up and walked to the window, looking out over the compound below. His posture was tense. Tom watched him closely, every nerve in his body on edge, waiting for the next move.

"How exactly did you get here?" Compton asked without turning around. His voice was casual, but Tom could hear the undercurrent of suspicion.

"I took a raft," Tom replied smoothly. He had anticipated this question. "From the mainland. It wasn't easy."

Compton turned to face him, his eyes sharp as ever. "That's a long way from the mainland to take a raft."

"As I said," Tom replied, "it wasn't easy."

"And you came alone?" Compton asked.

Tom nodded. "Just me."

The general stared at him for a moment, then

nodded toward the door. "Take him to a holding room," he ordered the guard standing by the entrance. "Until I decide what to do with him."

Tom remained still as the guard approached, grabbing his arm and pulling him up to his feet. He didn't resist, allowing himself to be led out of the office and down the narrow corridor to the small, windowless room that served as a temporary holding cell. The door closed behind him with a metallic clang, leaving him alone in the dim light.

Tom sat with his head in his hands, trying to quiet his racing thoughts. He couldn't stay in this room much longer—he had to get out and cause a distraction. He stood up, pacing the small room. After a few moments, he took a deep breath and collapsed to the floor, clutching his chest as though in pain.

He groaned, his breath coming in short, ragged gasps. "Help…please…"

The guard outside the door shifted, his shadow visible through the small window. For a moment, there was silence. Then, the door creaked open.

The guard stepped inside cautiously, his eyes narrowing as he approached. "What's going on?"

Tom gasped again, his hand pressed to his chest. "I think…my heart…" His voice trailed off as he slumped further to the floor, his breath shallow and labored.

The guard hesitated, taking a step closer. His hand hovered over his pistol, unsure what to do. Finally, the guard knelt beside him, reaching out to check his pulse.

That was all Tom needed. With lightning-fast reflexes, he shot out his hand, grabbing the guard's wrist and twisting it hard. The guard let out a surprised yelp, but it was quickly cut off as Tom slammed his other fist into the man's throat, cutting off his air supply.

The guard crumpled to the floor, gasping for breath. Tom didn't give him a chance to recover. He grabbed the guard's pistol and, with one clean motion, fired a single shot into the man's chest. He stood up, his chest heaving as he stared down at the body. He didn't have any time to spare.

He ran out of the room into the narrow corridor and back to Compton's office. He knew all too well what he had to do next. He stepped around Compton's desk, reached down, and opened a drawer.

"Alright, boys," he whispered to himself, "you're up."

He reached into the drawer and flipped a switch, sounding the alarms throughout the compound.

* * *

Jake crouched low in the dense underbrush, eyes locked on the open airfield that stretched before him. Several planes stood silently along the runway as if frozen in time. He couldn't help but wonder how such a massive operation had been pulled off without any sign of detection. Their resources, their coordination—it was unsettling. At the far end of the runway, three helicopters sat idle. Only one mattered to him. He could only hope that it was fueled up.

He wiped the sweat trickling down his face and raised his binoculars, scanning the field with a careful eye. Five guards. Two stood stationed near the helicopters, rifles slung across their shoulders, while three more patrolled the perimeter.

Then the alarms shattered the stillness. The sharp blare pierced through the air, and the guards reacted instantly, snapping to attention and sprinting toward the compound. The moment they disappeared into the distance, he moved.

He bolted from the cover of the trees, sprinting across the open airfield with every muscle coiled and ready. There was no time to think—just run. The distance to the helicopter closed quickly, the thudding of his boots nearly drowned out by the ringing alarms in the distance.

Jake reached the nearest helicopter and wasted no time. He leaped into the cockpit, crouching beside the controls. His eyes scanned the dashboard, fingers grazing the instruments as he checked for anything out of place. The layout was familiar enough—everything seemed operational, the systems responding to his touch as he quickly assessed the situation. Fuel levels, battery, ignition—it was all in order. All that was left to do was wait.

* * *

Carl moved with equal precision, each step calculated as he crossed the grassy field toward the munitions depot. The blaring alarm echoed in the distance, drilling into his mind and making his pulse race. His nerves were on edge, every instinct screaming for him to move faster, but he couldn't afford a single misstep. Not now. He forced himself to breathe steadily. Failure wasn't an option.

The moment he reached the depot, he yanked the door open. The scent of gunpowder hit him immediately, thick and acrid in the air. The large, dimly lit warehouse stretched out before him, rows of bombs stacked like sleeping giants—silent but full of devastating potential. Leftovers from Operation Impact. Carl only needed to rig one. Just one. That would be enough to ignite a chain reaction that would turn the entire stockpile into a firestorm.

He moved swiftly, pulling the tools from his backpack, his hands steady despite the adrenaline coursing through him. His fingers found the bomb, running over its surface as he assessed it. This was the one. He crouched down, isolating the wires, his mind focused. He reached into his bag and pulled out the timer, feeling its weight in his palm. Ten minutes, maybe fifteen, and everything in this place would go up in flames.

He started rewiring, each movement precise, no room for error. The ticking of his watch seemed to grow louder with each second that passed, pressing down on him. The seconds felt like a countdown in his own head. His hands worked quickly, attaching the timer and splicing the wires. The slightest mistake could be catastrophic.

"No mistakes," he echoed Tom's words.

As he finished wiring the last connection, he stood up and set the timer, watching the red digital numbers blink into life. His work was done. He needed to get to the helicopter fast.

* * *

Outside, Jake waited impatiently by the helicopter, his heart pounding. He scanned the treeline for any sign of Tom, his mind racing with worry. After what seemed like an eternity, movement caught his eye. Tom emerged from the trees. Jake felt a wave of relief wash over him, but it was short-lived.

"Going somewhere, Tom?" The voice froze him in place.

Tom's blood ran cold at the sound of Compton's voice. He turned slowly, his muscles tensing as he processed the scene unfolding before him. Compton stood at the edge of the airfield, a sinister grin on his face, and in his grasp was his son.

"Nick?" Tom whispered, the word barely escaping his lips. It was as though the ground had shifted beneath him. His son, alive?

Compton's grin widened as he held Nick by the collar, forcing him to his knees. "Surprised?" The general's voice was cold.

Nick's wide, terrified eyes met Tom's, and at that

moment, Tom felt something snap inside him. The weariness, exhaustion, and years of running and fighting vanished, replaced by a burning rage.

"Let him go, Compton," Tom growled. He took a step forward, his fists clenching at his sides. "This is between you and me. Let him go."

Compton shook his head slowly, his grip tightening on Nick. "Oh no, Tom. This is far bigger than you and me. This is about loyalty. This is about betrayal. You thought you could come here, play your little game, and walk away? I don't think so. You're going to watch your son die, just like you watched everything else crumble around you."

"Nick! Run!" Tom yelled.

In a burst of adrenaline, Nick twisted out of Compton's grasp. Compton stumbled briefly, caught off guard.

"Get to the helicopter now!" Tom yelled. "Jake! Get him out of here!"

"No!" Compton roared, raising his gun to fire.

Tom moved without thinking. He lunged at Compton, tackling him to the ground before the general could get a shot off. The two men hit the dirt with a thud, and the gun skidded across the ground, out of reach.

Compton reacted quickly, landing a hard punch to Tom's ribs, but Tom didn't feel the pain. All he felt was fury. He grabbed Compton by the collar and threw him to the side, rolling on top of him and pinning him down.

"You took my son!" Tom snarled, his fists crashing into Compton's face. "You took everything from me!"

Compton struggled beneath him, his hands clawing at Tom's arms, but Tom's grip was ironclad. The helicopter's blades began to whir to life in the background, the sound growing louder, drowning out the sounds of the struggle. Tom spared a glance toward them, relief flooding him for a brief moment.

But Tom couldn't leave yet. Not until he finished what he had started. With a surge of strength, Compton managed to twist out of Tom's grip, shoving him back and scrambling to his feet. Blood dripped from his mouth, his face bruised and swollen, but his eyes were alight with rage. He reached for the knife strapped to his belt, brandishing it as he squared off with Tom. Just then, Carl emerged from the treeline and rushed toward Compton.

"Carl! Get out of here!" Tom yelled.

But it was too late. Carl dove at Compton, and with one swift swing of the arm, the knife plunged into Carl's neck.

"NO!" Tom cried out as he watched Carl's body hit the ground.

"This ends now," Compton hissed, lunging forward with the blade.

Tom dodged the first swipe, his body moving on instinct. The two men circled each other like animals, both knowing that only one would walk away. The knife glinted in the dim light as Compton slashed again, this time grazing Tom's arm. Pain shot through Tom, but he barely registered it. His focus was on the knife, on the opening he needed. Compton was fast, but Tom was faster.

With a quick sidestep, Tom avoided another strike and grabbed Compton's wrist, twisting it hard until the knife clattered to the ground. Compton roared in frustration, but Tom drove his fist into the general's gut before he could react, knocking the wind out of him.

Compton stumbled back, gasping for air, but Tom didn't let up. He moved forward relentlessly, grabbing Compton by the throat and slamming him against a nearby tree. Compton's eyes bulged as Tom's grip tightened, his breath coming in short, desperate gasps.

"You don't get to hurt my family anymore," Tom growled. He squeezed harder, watching as the life drained from Compton's eyes. "This is for Nick."

With one final, brutal twist, Tom snapped Compton's neck. The general's body went limp in Tom's hands, and for a moment, there was silence. Tom let the body fall to the ground, his chest heaving with exertion. It was over. Compton was dead.

But as Tom stood there, staring down at the lifeless body of the man who had tormented him for so long, a realization hit him. The helicopter's blades were growing fainter. Jake had followed his orders and took Nick to safety. The helicopter rose higher and higher, disappearing into the distance. Tom stood alone on the empty airfield, the wind howling around him as the realization sank in. He wasn't getting off the island.

Jake looked over his shoulder as the helicopter sped away from the island. His hands gripped the controls tightly, his heart pounding. Nick sat beside him, trying to make sense of everything that just happened.

And then…the explosion.

A massive fireball erupted from the island, the shockwave rippling through the air and sending debris flying in every direction. Jake's breath caught in his throat as he watched the island crumble behind them, the buildings collapsing in on themselves, the entire landscape engulfed in flames. He didn't know what part of the island housed the rest of the corrupted officials but he knew one thing for sure…nobody was going to survive this.

"Dad?…" Nick's voice was small and frightened as he looked back at the island.

Jake closed his eyes briefly, a single tear slipping down his cheek.

Chapter 25

Emily woke up to Jake's warmth beside her, his arm draped loosely over her waist. His breathing was a soft rhythm that brought her comfort, and his chest's quiet rise and fall was a gentle reminder that they were still together. She lay there, savoring the calm before the day ahead, her fingers tracing faint patterns on his shoulder.

Jake stirred, his eyes fluttering open, and a sleepy smile pulled at the corners of his mouth. "Morning," he murmured, voice thick with sleep.

Emily smiled, brushing a few strands of his hair from his forehead. "Morning," she whispered. "It's early…but today's the day."

He stretched, blinking fully awake, the weight of her words sinking in. "Today's the day," he echoed, letting the thought linger.

"I love you," Emily said quietly.

Jake's eyes softened, his hand finding hers, fingers lacing together. "I love you too, Em."

They dressed and readied themselves, the air in the bunker buzzing with energy. A sense of nervous excitement had built since their plan spread. It wasn't just another day of survival but a leap into something new, a step toward a future beyond these walls.

Outside the meeting room, they met Frank, who was waiting. "You two ready?" he asked.

Jake chuckled. "As ready as we'll ever be."

Emily drew in a deep breath, nodding. "Let's do this."

They walked together to the main chamber, where everyone had gathered, their faces filled with anticipation, fear, and something more—hope. People of all ages who had come together in the darkest of times now stood side by side, ready to face the unknown world outside.

The hum of conversation quieted as Emily stepped to the front. For a moment, she took in the crowd, the faces of people who had become her family. She cleared her throat.

"These past two years have tested us in ways we never expected," she began. "We've lost people, we've faced unimaginable challenges, but we've survived. We're here today because of our strength, our resilience, and each other."

She glanced at Jake and Frank, drawing strength from their steady presence beside her.

"Today," she continued, "we're taking our first steps toward something new. I don't know what the future holds for us, but I know this—we're ready. We're stronger now; no matter what lies ahead, we'll face it together."

A ripple of murmurs spread through the crowd. With a nod to Jake, she signaled it was time. He moved to the control panel beside the massive steel doors, his hands steady as he entered the code to unlock them. The room held its breath, watching as he pressed the final button. Gears turned, mechanisms hummed, and with a deep creak, the doors began to part.

The light from outside was blinding, a burst of sunlight cutting through the dim, artificial lighting they had known for so long. For the first time in two years, the people of the bunker saw the sky.

Gasps filled the room, some shielding their eyes as they adjusted to the brightness. The air was fresh, carrying the scent of fresh grass and earth, the smell of life itself. Emily's heart swelled as she took her first breath of clean air, a rush of emotion bringing tears to her eyes.

Jake extended a hand to her, and she took it, her fingers threading through his as they entered the light together. Frank followed, and soon, the rest of the residents began to filter out of the bunker, their faces filled with awe for the world they saw anew.

Some dropped to their knees, overcome by the sheer beauty of the open sky. Others let out quiet gasps; hands lifted to the sun as if to absorb every bit of warmth and light they had missed. After so long in darkness, this was more than freedom—it was a rebirth. But the quiet reverie was interrupted by a question from someone in the crowd that hung heavy in the air:

"Where do we go now?"

A hush fell as the words settled, a reminder of reality. They had lost everything—their homes, families, and the lives they'd known. The world they had once known was now foreign to them.

Emily turned to the crowd. "The truth is, we don't have many options. The bunker is still here, and it's still a safe place for us. We don't have to stay locked inside anymore, but it's still our home."

Nods of understanding rippled through the crowd. The bunker had given them life and hope, and though they had a choice now to explore beyond it, the familiar walls had become more than just a refuge—they were part of their story.

In the following days, the residents spread out, reacquainting themselves with the outside world. Gardens began to take shape in patches of soil, makeshift gathering spots formed under the open sky, and shared meals became celebrations of life. The laughter returned, children ran and played, and the sound of joy replaced the quiet hum of survival.

Through it all, Jake continued his work, reaching out over the radio to other bunkers. His voice traveled through the airwaves, sending messages to nearby communities, and soon, responses trickled in. Word of their resilience and hope spread from bunker to bunker, each story adding to a survival network.

One night, as they stood together on the hillside overlooking the bunker, Jake wrapped an arm around her waist, pulling her close. The night air was cool, stars twinkling in a sky that felt vast and filled with possibility.

"Did you ever imagine we'd get here?" Emily asked. Jake looked down at her with soft eyes. "Maybe in my wildest dreams. But with you by my side, anything feels possible."

She leaned into him, her heart full, feeling a sense of peace that had been absent for so long. "What's next for us?" she asked.

Jake squeezed her hand. "I'm not sure," he replied. "But until we figure out what is out there, maybe we should stick around the bunker."

Emily looked up at him, nodding, a smile playing on her lips. "Yes," she said. "Let's stay here at the bunker."

Epilogue

Tom jolted awake, his heart pounding and his skin slick with sweat. Darkness pressed in around him, the air thick and suffocating. For a moment, he couldn't place where he was—the walls felt too close, the silence too eerie. He was disoriented, the remnants of his dream clinging to him like a heavy fog.

It had started so sweetly, so innocently—dinner with May and Nick. The three of them together, like old times, sitting at the kitchen table. May had been laughing, the sound light and musical, like wind chimes on a gentle breeze. Nick had been smiling, his small hands reaching across the table for bread, his face lighting up every time Tom passed him another piece. Tom had been content, the warmth of family wrapping around him like a comforting blanket. Everything had been perfect.

But lurking just beyond the edge of these beautiful moments, something had been wrong. Compton. He was there—watching. Waiting. Tom had seen him, his presence looming like a shadow at the edge of every happy memory. But May and Nick hadn't noticed. They hadn't seen the danger. Compton had stalked them through the dream, inching closer with every moment, his dark figure looming over them, always just out of reach. And then, just when Tom thought he could grab them, save them, pull them away from the danger— he'd woken up.

His breath came in ragged gasps as he sat up, wiping the sweat from his brow. The small cot creaked under his weight, and the metallic echo of his movement filled the cramped space around him. It was too dark, too quiet. The walls felt like they were closing in on him. He needed air. He needed to get out.

Stumbling out of the cot, his legs heavy and unsteady, Tom moved through the small space. His fingers grazed the cold metal walls as he made his way to the hatch. His fingers fumbled with the latch, his hands shaking from the adrenaline coursing through his veins. Finally, the hatch gave way, creaking as it swung open. A blinding shaft of sunlight poured into the bunker, momentarily disorienting him. Tom winced, shielding his eyes with his arm as he adjusted to the sudden brightness. The sunlight felt foreign after so many days in darkness, the heat of it warm against his skin. He took a deep breath, inhaling the fresh air, letting it fill his lungs.

Climbing out of the bunker, Tom stood in the open air, blinking against the bright light. His gaze fell on a large piece of debris floating in the water, half-submerged but still intact. He waded into the water and climbed on top of it. It was large enough to hold him, sturdy enough to stay afloat. It would have to do.

He sat for a moment, catching his breath. His muscles ached from the strain, his body still weak from everything he had endured. He picked up a piece of driftwood floating next to him and used it to start paddling out to sea. He had one last mission to complete.

"Hold on, Nick," he said out loud. "I'm coming home."

About the author:

Adam McKim was born and raised in a small town in Missouri, where he still lives today with his wife and son. He began writing in his early twenties and has authored a growing collection of poems and books. When he's not writing, he enjoys quiet moments with family and the continued pursuit of storytelling.